Killing the Kansas City Shuffle

MISS MARKHAM MYSTERY SERIES
BOOK THREE

DEBORAH DILKS

Library of Congress Control Number forthcoming: ____________________

ISBN (hardcover): 978-1-7330444-5-5

ISBN (paperback): 978-1-7330444-6-2

Killing the Kansas City Shuffle

MISS MARKHAM MYSTERY SERIES
BOOK THREE

DEBORAH DILKS

Kansas City Shuffle Book Reviews:

"Killing the Kansas City Shuffle puts Miss Markham in the middle of the corruption, the Mob, and the murders in this exciting look into Kansas City during the early 1930s. A mystery with a twist!"

— Joyce Henkins

"I loved this book, Killing the Kansas City Shuffle, and hated to see it end. I savored reading the last chapter."

— Kristie Zorn

"I loved how Deloris finds clever ways to solve crimes as she navigates through this story filled with colorful characters. This visual and delicious tale will leave you craving for more. I highly recommend this cozy Kansas City mystery series with author Deborah Dilks. It's a great story and I loved the references."

— Rosie Russell of "Books by Rose"

"I really loved this book and was sad for it to end. I was waiting for [Deloris] to get a job as a detective next."

— Stella All

"I really liked the book." **— Julie Casey**

"This was really good! I enjoyed 'Deloris' / Doris and since I knew her, I could "see' her doing these things!! Thank you [for asking me to beta read]!!"

— Judy Pelletier

"Another fun read with just enough history to help create a visual image of the setting."

—Gail Metcalf Schartel

"Pugnacious and plucky Miss Markham immerses you in the 1930s criminal world of Kansas City as she works to solve the murder of con-man Slick Sam Sloan—master of the Kansas City Shuffle. Find out if you will be taken in by the really big con of the story—a compelling read!"

— Jo Ann Day

Acknowledgements

Thank you to my family and friends for their support, suggestions, and help. I especially want to recognize the following for their help, input and information: Stella All, Angie Martell, Mary and Greg Hunsucker from V's Restaurant, Johnny Holiday and Benny Merrick with the Kansas City Gangster Tour (kcganstertour.com). Frank Hayde's book, *Mafia and the Machine*, also helped us understand and come to know some of the gangsters from that period. Also, this book would not be possible without my support system, my Beta Readers Kristie Zorn, Joyce Henkins, Julie Casey, Gail Schartel, Jo Ann Day, Racheal Shatswell, Rosie Russell, Judy Pelletier.

A special thank you to my husband, Elden Dilks. Without your support, book suggestions, cooking delicious meals, and occupying our dog, none of my books would ever be written. Thank you.

Book Cover Drawn by Maia Leonard, Copy Editing by Sara McClure, and Book Cover and Formatting by Carolyn Day.

This book is dedicated to Doris Markham Swinney, my inspiration, role model, and mother. Yes, she is a real person who may not have lived all of these adventures, but with her adventurous spirit, she could have! Some events are true that she experienced.

More Information

Visit my websites at MissMarkhamMysteries.com and DeborahDilks.com, or Facebook pages: "Juliet E. Sidonie, Author," and "Deborah Dilks, Writer" for more historical tidbits, newspaper articles that inspired some stories, and other interesting information.

Contact me at delorismarkham09@gmail.com.

Table of Contents

Preface

The Kansas City Shuffle is a con game played on a mark (victim). As in a magic trick, everyone is looking one way when the action is happening elsewhere.

Grifter (noun) is a person who engages in petty or small-scale swindling. Slick Sam Sloan was a grifter — a mercurial man who was a quick thinker.

Feint (adjective) Feigned; counterfeit (of attack) directed toward a different part from the intended strike. Synonyms are trick, ploy, ruse, maneuver, plead false ignorance. There are other definitions and uses for this word, but for this book, these fit nicely.

In days gone by, people still had to be careful of scams such as the Kansas City Shuffle, but their resources were limited and not as sophisticated. Today, we are wary of scams and people phishing for information through email, phone call, text, or social media message. Scammers may use AI to falsify who is contacting the mark, or capture the images and voice of a person to fool their family and friends.

Songs and movies have been written about the Kansas City Shuffle. Now we will attempt to write about a book about the Killing of the Kansas City Shuffle.

Be sure to check out the Additional Information in the back of the book. And List of Characters.

List of Characters

DELORIS "DEDE" MARKHAM–A brunette with violet eyes, a knockout figure and good-looking gams, Deloris knows there's more to the world than the small town she grew up in. Her friends and family call her DeDe because, as a child, she stuttered, and this is how she said her name.

FRANCESCA "FRANNY" CASCIOLA–Cook at the Venetian Gardens Restaurant.

ENZO CASCIOLA–Franny's son who also works at the Venetian Gardens.

CONSTANCE "CONNIE" BINAGGIO–Married to Nino and manages the Venetian Gardens.

NINO BINAGGIO–One of Poppy's Paradise Park owners and owner of the Venetian Gardens.

SAL BINAGGIO–Works at the Venetian Gardens behind the counter, but looks more like a bodyguard. He is Nino's brother.

OLIVIA FONTANA–Franny Casciola's sister who also works at the Venetian Gardens.

ANGELO "ANGEL" MARTINELLI–Owner of Indiana Gardens Restaurant and the Snooker Club next door.

SICILIA MARTINELLI–Owner and manager of Indiana Gardens Restaurant.

MARY LOUISA MARTINELLI–Angel and Sicilia's daughter-in-law.

NINA MARTINELLI–Angelo and Sicilia Martinelli's granddaughter.

STELLA MARTINELLI–Angelo & Sicilia Martinelli's granddaughter, who also works with Deloris at Poppy's Paradise Park.

COTILLA "TILLY" ROSS–Girlfriend to both Sam and Jules, who is a singer with the band.

LILLIBETH "LILLY" ROSS–Works with Deloris at Venetian Gardens.

SLICK SAM SLOAN–A grifter or a con man who liked to pull the Kansas City Shuffle on unsuspecting marks.

JULIUS T. STANFORD II (JULIUS)–Lumber Tycoon.

JULIUS T. STANFORD III (JULES)–Heir apparent of Stanford Lumber and Sugarhouse Syndicate

~ Kansas City Police Department Employees ~

JIM "BIG JIM" ANDERSON–A detective at the Kansas City Police Department, over six feet tall with brown hair and green eyes. He is a former Marine who has mastered the art of the intimidating stare.

CAROLYN BECHTEL–Assistant coroner at the Kansas City Police Department. Carolyn is an attractive woman with short brown hair and soft blue eyes.

TED COX–Front desk sergeant at the police station.

AUSTIN MARTIN–Childhood friend of Deloris's who graduated from Jameson the year before her. Their mothers were good friends, so Austin and Deloris grew up together more like brother and sister. Austin's goal is to become a tenured Kansas City, Missouri, police detective. He is six feet tall, has blonde hair, blue eyes, and a square jaw.

MARY VIRGINIA MILES–Manager of the KCPD switchboard and Deloris's supervisor.

~ Thelma's Boarders and Friends ~

ANNIE BAILEY–Has a quiet demeanor and loves finding out the story behind something. She is a pretty girl with a cute round face, a few freckles sprinkled across her nose, blue eyes, and curly strawberry blonde hair that she wears short trying to control it. Annie works at *The Kansas City Post* newspaper.

GRACE "GRACIE" BURNETT–A cool, calm, and collected young woman with long blonde hair, blue eyes and a warm, glowing personality. When everyone else panics, Gracie calms the waters. She takes classes at the University of Kansas City and works at the KCPD switchboard weekends.

LEON IRAKLIDIS–Deloris's boyfriend and soda fountain repair fellow.

LEOTA JONES–Boards at Thelma's boarding house, and has brown eyes and short, straight mousy brown hair that she still wears in a 1920s pixie style. She works as a maid at the President Hotel and babysits Thelma's daughters while Thelma works.

THELMA WEBB–Deloris's twice-divorced older sister who has two children. Thelma works nights at the Egg Factory and, to help make ends meet, she rents rooms in her house to single females. Thelma is short and round, with short red hair that she recently cut, reinventing herself.

EDITH WELLINGTON–Big Jim's girlfriend and Thelma's newest boarder. Edith is a chemistry teacher at the University of Kansas City.

LES WELLS–Deloris's boyfriend from Independence.

~ Deloris's Co-workers at the Kansas City Police Department's Switchboard and Poppy's Paradise Park ~

BEVERLY "BOO"–Deloris's co-worker.

JOYCE–Deloris's co-worker.

LOREDA "LORI"–Deloris's co-worker.

PAM–Deloris's co-worker.

TRUDIE–Deloris's coworker at Poppy's and good friends with Stella.

VIRGIL–Deloris's coworker at Poppy's at the soda fountain

Prologue

Sam Sloan, or Slick Sam, as his friends called him, was a conman. His father was a conman. His grandfather was a conman, and so on down the line; he came by his skills naturally. Finding a mark in 1931 was easy because people were hurting financially, even the rich ones, and they were desperate to make an easy buck anywhere they could find it.

Sam was at his usual haunt, an Italian restaurant in Kansas City, Missouri, on Grand Avenue, looking for his next mark, Julius T. Stanford III, a fellow who was no stranger to the gambling scene. He always studied his victims carefully before engaging them in the scam, or "the game," as he liked to call it. He knew their likes, their dislikes, their passions, and their shortcomings as well as he knew his own.

As he sat at his favorite table in the back near the kitchen, reading the newspaper and sipping his coffee, the waitress came by.

"Would you like for me to freshen that up for you?"

Sam looked up into the young woman's violet eyes and almost lost himself in their depths. He had never seen violet eyes before. Recovering quickly, he pushed his coffee cup closer to her and said, "Sure, doll. I haven't seen you here before. Did you just step out of my dreams? Am I dreaming?"

Deloris Markham smiled cautiously.

"I haven't seen you here before. What's your story?" he asked.

"Tonight is my first night," she answered as she refilled his coffee. "Do you want to order?"

"Naw sweetheart. I just want to get lost in your eyes. You are an angel. Am I dead? Did I die and somehow went to heaven?"

He reached for her hand, but she quickly avoided his grasp, saying, "Okay, you are very much alive and this isn't heaven," she replied, laughing.

"How's about you and me getting better acquainted, doll?" he asked, looking her up and down. "I got two tickets to the Pla-Mor's formal reopening tomorrow night. We can dance the night away. Whaddaya say?"

"No thanks," Deloris replied, keeping her eyes on the now-full coffee mug.

"Ah, come on, sugar. Don't be so quick to say no. You really don't want to pass up this once-in-a-lifetime opportunity, do you?" Sam pleaded. "I can be very entertaining."

"I'm sure you can. Did you plan to order something?" Deloris persisted as she sat the coffeepot down and pulled out her order pad and pencil from her apron pocket.

"Nah, I just come here for the coffee and the scenery," he said, winking. "How about tomorrow night?"

"Save it, Joe. I already have a boyfriend and we have plans." He didn't need to know that she actually had two boyfriends, because he might take that as an invitation for him to be number three.

"Too bad, and my name is Sam. Sam Sloan. Not Joe. How about you ditch him and go with me? I could show you a real good time."

"Oh, I'm sure you could," Deloris tossed the comment over her shoulder as she walked away to greet the patrons at a table near the front of the restaurant.

Sam called after her, "Well, dollface, if you decide to dump that boyfriend of yours, remember we could be having a good time at the Pla-Mor."

Sam watched her walk away until his attention was drawn to the couple who had just walked in. There he was, the man Sam was waiting to see, standing across the room from him. Julius T. Stanford III, who went by the name Jules, was the heir apparent to a lumber tycoon. On his arm was one of the most beautiful women Sam had ever seen: a blonde bombshell who reminded him of Jean Harlow from the movie pictures. She was fire and ice rolled into one. She was the kind of woman men might commit murder for. He wanted to know her name. No, he reasoned, he had to be careful. Beautiful women were his passion—and his downfall. Every time he tried to hook up with one, he wound up on the losing end of the relationship. Married twice and divorced twice, Sam didn't have a penny to his name after being taken to the cleaners when the wives were finished with him. That is why he had to step-up his game picking higher-end chumps.

Sam first heard about Jules when he read about him winning a tidy sum of money at the Riverside Racetrack. From that information, he knew Jules liked to gamble, making him an easy mark. Jules was close friends with Johnny Lazia, and the two hung out at the Riverside Park Jockey Club's Racetrack. They were more like brothers than friends, really. Sam kept a little black book with information on all of his marks, and he had gone to the library to read what he could about Jules' life in past issues of the newspapers. Since he was considered one of Kansas City's elite, finding him in the newspapers was easy. His father was often in pictures rubbing elbows with E.F. Swinney, President of the First National Bank, and R.A. Long, another successful lumberman.

The news press was there to capture every minute of Jules' life, too. He graduated from Pembroke School and was an avid polo and lacrosse player. Jules went to Harvard majoring in business, and his parents were so proud that they threw him a large party at the Riverside Park Jockey Club to celebrate his return home. Since the party, he seldom appeared in the newspapers—just a mention here or there when he attended some girl's soiree or an event at the jockey club. Now, Sam had to put on his investigative hat and dig for more information. He had a buddy, Ronnie the Runt, who worked as a busboy at Riverside. Sam promised him 5% of the take from the game, and Ronnie had come through, telling Sam that he overheard Jules talking about going to Venetian Gardens tonight.

Snapping back to reality, Sam quickly put the newspaper up to his face and pretended to be reading it. He wasn't ready to introduce himself to Jules. Soon the time would be right and he'd make his move, but right now he'd watch and learn.

However, this woman was a fresh development. Was Jules' girl making eyes at him behind her boyfriend's back? He eyed her around the edge of the newspaper. Here she was, a knock-out and out of his league, but how could he resist? Sam smiled at her and nodded in recognition of her attention. She smiled back with a slight nod of her own. "Oh boy, am I in trouble?" Sam whispered to himself. He gulped and watched her closely. She seemed to steal a glance at him every chance she got. He had to get to know her and why she was flirting with him. Suddenly, Sam noticed someone he didn't want to see come into the restaurant. Folding his paper, he made a hasty retreat out the back door. He would ask around and catch up with this doll again.

Chapter One

A Few Weeks Earlier

On Sunday, August 9, 1931, Deloris Markham arrived back in Kansas City a little later than she thought she would, but she couldn't help it. She had to know who the murderer was in her hometown, Jameson, Missouri. Besides, the train trip home had a pleasant surprise of Les Wells on the same train. They spent the time talking about what happened, and by the time they arrived at Union Station, she and Les had a date for the following weekend. Deloris hated to leave for her room at her sister's when she and Les arrived at Union Station, but it was getting late and she needed to get to bed. She worked mornings Monday thru Friday at the Kansas City Police Department switchboard, and weekends at Poppy's Paradise Park. At least that was the plan until Labor Day.

As she settled into bed, Deloris's worries overcame her exhaustion. Her weekend job at Poppy's was winding down for the end of the summer season in just three weeks. She worried about finding another part-time job to take her through the winter since the Depression made finding a full-time job very difficult. At almost nineteen years old, her options were a little slim, especially with her limited experience. From there her thoughts wandered back to Jameson and the Jameson Picnic. She hadn't quite come to terms with the surprising way things had ended. As she lay there, she tossed and turned and turned and tossed, going over and over each worry and concern in her head.

After lying awake for a while, Deloris mumbled to herself, "This isn't working." She got up and wrote a few thoughts and ideas down, hoping to clear them from her head so she could focus on relaxing and sleeping. That's when she decided to talk to Austin Martin, a KCPD detective and a long-time friend from Jameson, and ask him how he settled his mind in order to move on to the next case.

She picked up an old newspaper and read it, hoping it would tire her eyes enough for sleep. She read about a woman who shot her husband over a bridge game. "Well, that's not helping," she groaned, putting the newspaper down and climbing back into bed.

As she finally drifted off to sleep, Deloris dreamed of her hometown, where everyone was playing in a bridge tournament. One of the husbands got into an argument with his wife, accusing her of messing up her bid with one no trump. As he stood in front of her, arm raised to hit her, she produced a gun and shot him. But no one else reacted; they continued to play as if nothing happened. Deloris tried to get their attention to help the dying man, but no one moved. She tried shaking one man to alert him, but that's when her alarm went off.

Deloris awoke with a headache after only a few hours' sleep, and that dream hadn't helped her get any rest. She didn't feel like going to work, but she had to. There on the table next to her bed was the list she wrote the night before, but it was just gibberish. She rubbed her eyes, amused that it had made perfect sense when she wrote things down last night.

Deloris dressed and went downstairs, where she found her sister, Thelma, who ran the boarding house where she lived, making coffee.

"You're up mighty early," Thelma commented as she

filled the glass scoop with coffee, then scattered the contents around the filter in the top of the coffeepot. When she put the coffee pot on the gas stove burner and lit the fire under it, she glanced at Deloris, then turned to grab the iron skillet and start breakfast.

"I couldn't sleep," Deloris answered, shaking her head.

"What's got you up all night?"

"Oh, I keep thinking about how things ended up in Jameson, and then there's the fact I need to find another job for the winter."

"You need to put everything that happened up in Jameson out of your mind. What is done is done. Move on."

"I know," Deloris groaned.

Times were tough and most people had to work two jobs to make ends meet. Thelma and Deloris were no exception. Working two jobs was a necessity to keep food on the table, pay bills and simply survive. For additional funds, Thelma also turned her home into a boarding house for females only. She had five rooms, but now there were only four boarders, counting Deloris, with one vacancy.

"So, what's new with you?" Deloris asked her older sister.

"I met someone at the lunch counter and we are dating," Thelma said, slightly blushing.

"That's great. Tell me all about him," Deloris encouraged.

"He is a police officer with the Kansas City, Kansas Police Department."

"Really? Austin might know him. When do I get to meet him?"

"Not so fast, little sister. I don't want to scare him off."

"Maybe we can go on a double date sometime with my new

boyfriend, Les." Deloris said with a slight smile.

Somehow, with two jobs, two daughters, and a boarding house to run, Thelma found the time to have a new boyfriend. Deloris already liked him, because he was a switch from the losers she had been with before.

Leota Jones, another of Thelma's renters, came down the stairs at that point. Without a word to the sisters, she made herself some toast and quickly left for her job as a maid at the President Hotel. For some reason, she never seemed to like Deloris, but never expressed why. So, Deloris just shrugged it off as her extreme shyness.

One by one, Thelma's other two renters joined them in the kitchen. Annie Bailey was a reporter for The Kansas City Post newspaper, and Gracie Burnett was a college student at Kansas City Junior College who worked weekends at the Kansas City Police Department switchboard. Annie asked Deloris about her week in Jameson and Deloris related her experiences there with her and Gracie. Then Gracie told them about her classes that she would be starting in a week. She was especially excited to meet the new chemistry teacher. "She's a female," she exclaimed. All of my other professors are male, even the literature teacher, and to have a female in the sciences is very rare. After breakfast, Deloris and the other girls cleaned up and Thelma got her daughters ready to go to the park to play.

When Deloris got to the police station, she walked in with her coworker, Pam. They clocked in and put their purses in their lockers.

Pam asked, "How was your weekend?"

"It was okay," Deloris said with a shrug.

Concerned, Pam stopped and turned to her friend sensing something was wrong in her response. "You look like you had a rough night. Didn't you have a good weekend up in your hometown?"

"I just had a restless night."

"What's got you up all night, sweetie?" Pam asked, touching Deloris's shoulder gently.

Not able to hold it in any longer, Deloris blurted out, "You'll never believe what happened." Just then, three other co-workers walked in and joined the conversation.

"What's happening? What's wrong, honey?" Joyce asked, noticing the pained expression on Deloris's face. Lori and Boo (whose real name was Beverly) nodded with concerned looks on their faces.

"Yes, what's wrong, Deloris?" they echoed Joyce's question.

"Oh, Deloris here was just going to tell me about her weekend," Pam answered with a wave of her hand. "Go on, Deloris, we're listening."

Before she could continue, Mary Virginia Miles, their office manager, entered the room from her office. "Girls, it's eight o'clock. Are we ready to work?" It was a half inquiry and half command.

"Yes," they all answered in unison as they walked to their respective workstations. Each of them rolled out their secretarial type chairs, sat down, adjusted their pillows brought from home for comfort, and put their headphones on.

As soon as Mary Virginia was back in her office, Joyce leanedover from her station. "Go on Deloris, tell us what happened before it gets busy," she whispered loudly.

Deloris related her story about the body found and the

long-lost girl returning home. She left out the part about how it ended, though. Pam, Joyce, Lori, and Boo sat in complete silence with their mouths agape.

Pam was the first to find her voice. Shaking her head, she said, "So, is this common in your little hometown to find dead bodies buried in the park? I can't imagine this happening in my hometown."

"No," Deloris answered, slightly annoyed. "This is totally out of character for my hometown. I couldn't imagine it happening in Jameson either, but you never know what will drive people to murder."

"Do they know who did it?" Lori asked.

"They have someone in custody." She paused before continuing, "Someone I never imagined would be charged with the murder or to be involved."

"Do you think that person really was the murderer?" Joyce pressed.

"I can't say," Deloris responded mysteriously, not meeting anyone's eye.

"Can't or won't?" Pam asked.

At that moment, the switchboard lit up like a Christmas tree with a call for each person.

Boo plugged her line in first. "Kansas City Police Department, what is your emergency, please? Your car won't start?" She chuckled, "Ma'am, you need to ring up a mechanic, for that, not the police."

"Kansas City Police Department. What is your emergency, please?" Joyce answered. "A tree pruner fell from a tree? Do you need an ambulance?"

Pam answered, "Kansas City Police Department, what is

your emergency, please? You found a car sticking out of the Kaw River? Where? Kansas City, Kansas? You should ask the operator for the Kansas City, Kansas Police Department. No ma'am, you called the Kansas City, Missouri Police Department. Here, let me connect you."

"Kansas City Police Department, what is your emergency please?" Eyes widening at the caller's response, Lori asked, "You think there is a bank robbery taking place? Which bank?"

At that, Deloris started to say something when her board lit up, too. "Kansas City Police Department, what is your emergency, please? A bank robbery? Which bank? Yes, I believe someone else reported the robbery, too. Oh, you were just preparing to go into the bank, but went to the drugstore down the street instead to make this call? Yes, sir, but can you tell me how many robbers are in the bank? Yes, okay. Thank you. We'll send someone to check it out right away."

Deloris picked up the telephone receiver and called down to the front desk. "There is a reported bank robbery at the Fidelity Saving & Trust Company. The caller saw four robbers, three inside and one outside in a car."

Hanging up, she turned to her co-workers, giving a collective sigh of relief with all calls answered and processed.

Joyce leaned in again. "So, Deloris, are you planning to go back up to your hometown soon?"

"Not for a while. Why do you ask?"

"Well, it doesn't sound like you're satisfied with the results of the murder investigation up there."

"Oh, I'm still just a little shocked at the whole situation," Deloris answered, fiddling with the cord of her headset. It was just a little lie, but she wasn't going to discuss the whole incident here and now.

"Okay, well, if you need to talk, I'm here and I'm all ears," Joyce offered, seeing that Deloris wasn't comfortable talking about it any further. She turned back to her workstation to prepare for the next call.

The rest of the morning was fairly busy, and when Deloris clocked out for lunch, she went down the stairs to see her friend, Austin Martin. She wanted to get his opinion on the events in Jameson.

"Time for lunch," she stated as she breezed right by the front desk sergeant, Ted Cox. He'd grown accustomed to Deloris's knack for getting by him, so without even looking up, he motioned broadly that she could walk on into the detective's room.

Austin looked up as she entered and smiled. "Hey DeDe, what brings you down here?"

"I just stopped to see if you want to go to lunch," she said downheartedly.

"Sure, let me just wrap up this paperwork and I'll be with you in a New York minute. Where'd you want to go?"

"Whatcha working on?" Shaking her head, she added, "Oh, never mind."

Sensing something was wrong, since she usually persisted in being nosey, he said, "What's wrong, DeDe?"

"I'll tell you about it on the way to lunch. How about the Dove Cafe over on 8th and Main?"

"Sounds good to me." He picked up a pen and wrote a few more notes on the stack of papers in front of him as Deloris waited.

Austin signed off on the report and stood up, taking it to

the police captain's desk. Coming back, he grabbed his hat and said, "Let's fly."

As they walked the few blocks to the restaurant, Deloris asked, "How do you handle cases where you know the wrong person is charged with the crime?"

"Does this have something to do with the murder up in Jameson?" he asked.

"Yes," she replied as they entered the cafe and found a table.

"Tell me all about it." Austin listened closely to what she had to say as they sat at the cafe. Then he said, "Let me get this straight. You have someone who confessed to the murder, even though you know he isn't guilty. It sounds like the sheriff knows that too. If he accepts the confession, then you need to do the same and let it go."

"I know, but ..."

"Look, if it will make you feel any better, I'll talk with the sheriff the next time I go up home and just make sure the case is closed, and he is satisfied with the confession," Austin offered.

"You'd do that for me? That'd be swell. Thank you," she said, as she cut into the ravioli on her plate.

"Don't mention it. Now let's eat before lunchtime is over." Austin put a mouthful of spaghetti in his mouth and closed his eyes in appreciation of the flavors.

When Deloris and Austin finished their lunch, he dropped her off at her sister's boarding house before returning to the police station. "Are you going to be okay?"

"Oh yes, I just needed to talk to you. I hoped you'd help me with it."

Entering the boarding house, Deloris closed the door quietly because her sister, Thelma, was asleep in the back bedroom. Thelma always slept in the afternoons when she got home from the lunch counter, so when everyone entered the house, they tried to be as quiet as a mouse.

Deloris tiptoed up the stairs to her room. Looking at herself in the mirror over the dresser, she realized just how tired she looked. She looked at her alarm clock: one o'clock. "Maybe a quick nap," she mused. Stretching out on the bed, she thought about what Austin said, and took his advice to relax and just let it go. What was done was done and she couldn't change it, nor was she sure she wanted to change it now. Besides, it was in Austin's hands. With the murder and confessions out of her mind, she was asleep almost instantly. She woke up early the next morning feeling better and rested, after sleeping from the previous afternoon until that next morning. However, six in the morning was earlier than usual for her. She decided to get dressed, anyway.

Heading downstairs and into the dining room, Deloris was greeted by Thelma and Annie.

"There she is! How are you doing, sleepyhead?" Thelma chortled. "We rarely see you down here this early and when we do, you aren't too coherent wandering around in your nightgown searching for coffee."

"You guys let me sleep?" Deloris asked, taking a mug to pour some coffee.

"We figured you needed it," Annie replied.

Gracie entered the room and added, "We peeked in at you a time or two, but you were sound asleep. So yes, we let you sleep."

"Thank you. I guess I did need it."

Deloris left early for her job at the switchboard. She didn't intend to be early, but because she was wide awake, up and around, she decided she might as well catch the first bus and go to work. Unsurprisingly, she was the first one there, and startled the two girls who worked the night shift. She still didn't know their names, only having a passing acquaintance with them. Deloris knew she couldn't handle the midnight shift, and they looked like they had had a busy night. She didn't know how her sister did it at the egg factory.

"Oh good. Someone is here. We'll turn it over to you," one of them said, and before Deloris could protest or say anything about the time, they waved a quick goodbye and exited the building as fast as they could, even though their shift wasn't officially over for another thirty minutes.

Deloris shook her head as she walked back to the little hallway and hung her jacket on the hook. Glancing at the time clock, she thought about clocking in early, but knew it would mess things up on her time worked, so she didn't. She needed to wait until 8 o'clock to time in. Putting her purse in her locker, she filled the coffeepot and put it on the little stove in the small kitchen area to percolate. When it finished, she poured herself a cup of coffee and walked to her station at the switchboard. Sitting in the swivel chair, she turned to face the monstrosity of a switchboard. It was five times the size of the one in Jameson, where she covered it for Austin's mother when she needed to run errands. No lights were on or blinking, but she knew that soon the switchboard would be lit up like Electric Park and the quiet would be over. Hearing someone approaching in the hallway, she swiveled her chair around to face the door to see who would arrive next. It was no surprise that Mary Virginia was the first person to enter.

Mary Virginia stopped just inside the door, shocked to see Deloris. "You're here mighty early," she commented suspiciously.

"I finally got a good night's sleep for once, and I woke up early," Deloris said with a smile.

Looking around, Mary Virginia asked, "Where are the other two girls?"

"Oh, they left just as you arrived," Deloris lied, not wanting to rat them out.

Joyce and Pam arrived a few minutes later. They had apparently been talking on the way in, but when they saw Deloris sitting there, their conversation stopped.

"What are you doing here so early?" Pam inquired, seeing the coffee that she usually made was already done.

"I was just telling Mrs. Miles that I got a good night's sleep. I was going to take a quick nap yesterday afternoon, but slept straight through and everyone at home just let me sleep! So, since I awoke early, I decided to come in to work," she explained brightly.

"Good for you. I knew you were tired yesterday," Joyce said.

"Yes, I guess I needed the extra sleep," Deloris said, nodding her head. "I'm feeling much better now."

When Lori and Boo arrived, Lori asked the same question, "Deloris, what are you doing here so early?"

Deloris gave her the same response. The morning went quickly, with the phones constantly ringing. Actually, the next few weeks were so busy that before Deloris knew it, it was Labor Day weekend.

Chapter Two

Good Connections

Everything was happening too fast. The days were rushing by to Deloris's last day at Poppy's Paradise Park. Before she knew it, the calendar turned to Friday, September 4th. On Monday, her job at Poppy's Paradise Park working at the soda fountain would end, and she still didn't know what she was going to do for a second job. On Sunday, she would grab a newspaper and start looking again since Sunday's paper always had the most help wanted advertisements.

Friday evening at Poppy's was very busy with a constant stream of customers coming in for ice cream or a soda fountain drink. When closing time finally came, Deloris took a broom from the back room and started sweeping the leaves that had blown in the door. Realizing she forgot to get the dustpan, she went back to retrieve it.

As Deloris reentered the room, the bell over the door tinkled, and she looked up to see Mr. O'Brien, her supervisor, walk in.

"How did everything go in here?" he queried.

"Business has been crazy. I guess with the Ringling Brothers Circus here, we attracted more customers than usual. I hardly had time to think!" Deloris said, leaning on the broom. "I like it when customers are a little more dispersed. It gives me time to clean everything up and straighten the tables and chairs in-between but tonight was a constant rush. I didn't have time to even plan my next move."

"Yes, I presume you are correct about the circus," Mr. O'Brien said, looking around the slightly disheveled soda shop. "Oh, since you are here, can I cash out with you?" Deloris asked quickly before he could comment on the mess.

"Certainly." He walked to the front door and locked it. "Where's Virgil?"

"He took the trash to the dumpster."

"I see," Mr. O'Brien said. "I guess it was so busy, he didn't have time to clean either?"

"Yes, it was that busy," Deloris said. "He worked the soda fountain while I took the ice cream orders. He is a good helper," she added, not wanting to get Virgil into any trouble. She walked to the cash register and took the money out of the drawer. She took out one stack of bills and coins out at a time to keep them in order. She placed them on the counter behind her where Mr. O'Brien sat, and he began counting the money and writing the amount on a pad of paper. Deloris watched him count it before he put it in the cash bag.

"Speaking of planning your next move, what are you going to do when we close Monday?" he asked.

"I don't know. That is what I need to think about. I guess I'll get a Sunday newspaper and see what jobs are out there."

"You've done a great job here, especially when we were shorthanded and then with training a new employee," Mr. O'Brien said with a smile. "You brought Virgil up to speed quickly. If you need a reference, I'm happy to provide one."

"Thank you very much, Mr. O'Brien. I will take you up on that offer."

"Okay," he said, and knocked the counter with his knuckles as if to put a period at the end of his statement. He swiveled the stool around, arose from his seat, and put the cash bag under his arm. As he walked out, he paused at the door and said, "Good night, Miss Markham."

"Good night, Mr. O'Brien, and thank you again, sir." Deloris resumed her sweeping. Just as she finished and went to the back room to put the broom and dustpan away, the bell tinkled again.

"Why didn't Mr. O'Brien relock the door?" she muttered to herself. From the back room she yelled, "I'm sorry, we're closed!"

Hearing no answer, Deloris peeked around the door to see a man standing there dressed in a finely tailored Italian suit. She recognized him immediately as Nino Binaggio, the main owner of Poppy's Paradise Park, with who knows how many silent partners. She couldn't imagine what he was doing in the soda fountain and hoped she wasn't in any kind of trouble. She never talked to him before. When she had problems, she always went to Mr. O'Brien.Deloris gulped. "May I help you?"

"Are you Deloris Markham?" the man asked, eyeing her carefully.

"I am," she answered, smoothing her red and white stripped apron that covered the white dress of her uniform. Then she checked her red and white stripped garrison hat to make sure it was straight.

"I'm Nino. Nino Binaggio," he said as he extended his hand to shake hers.

Gingerly, she reached her hand forward.

He took a seat at the nearest stool and said, "I've heard from your supervisor, O'Brien, all summer of all the good things you've done for Poppy's this year and he just told me that you are looking for a job. I'm here to offer you one."

Relieved, she smiled broadly, but tried to contain her excitement, "Really? Oh, my goodness, that is wonderful."

"Yes, well, you've earned a lot of respect here, and I presume you will bring the same professionalism to this next job." He crossed his arms. "How old are you, if you don't mind me asking?"

"I'm eighteen, but I'll be nineteen in a couple of weeks," she quickly added, hoping that her age wouldn't be a problem.

"I see. We'll put you to work in the restaurant."

"What hours are you looking for?" she asked.

"Friday, Saturday and Sunday nights, 4 o'clock to midnight."

"What is the pay? If I may ask," she added.

"It pays twenty-seven dollars a week. Nine dollars a day, plus tips."

"Where, may I ask, is this restaurant?"

"Oh yes. It is the Venetian Gardens, located on the west side of Grand Avenue between 7th and 8th."

"What do I need to do to get started?"

A little surprised by her forthrightness, Nino raised an eyebrow and uncrossed his arms before he answered, "Right to the point. I like a person who asks all the right questions." He stood up and handed her a slip of paper. "Show up this Tuesday about two o'clock and ask to see Connie Binaggio, my wife. Tell her Nino sent you."

"That sounds wonderful. I'll be there! Thank you."

He smiled, nodded, and left. "That made my day," Deloris thought to herself as she resumed her clean-up. "Presuming his wife likes me and hires me." She couldn't wait to tell Thelma and the girls.

After a few more minutes, Virgil finally came back into the shop. "Where have you been?" Deloris demanded.

"I ran into Mr. O'Brien and he told me about a job opening," Virgil explained, shutting the door behind him. "He recommended me to the owners."

"You, too? Where is the job? What will you be doing?"

"It's at Nichol's Lunch Counter. They're going to start me out as a dishwasher." Virgil began straightening tables and putting up the chairs.

"Which one?"

"The one at 311 East 10th. He said that I might be moved to the one at 39th and Summit later."

"That's what I like about working here," Deloris said, starting to sweep again. "Once you're in, they take care of you."

"Do you have a job, yet?" Virgil asked. "Haven't had a chance to ask all night with it so busy."

"Mr. Binaggio came in while you were gone and just offered me one!"

"That's great."

Outside the gate of Poppy's Paradise Park sat a black 1929 Model A Ford Roadster Coupe with Les Wells, Deloris's new boyfriend inside. Even though it was only their third official date, it didn't feel like he was a new acquaintance because of the adventures she got him involved in at the picnic.

"Hello, Deloris," Les said with a cheery grin.

"Thank you for picking me up here," she said, returning the smile.

"No problem. Where shall we go?" he asked.

"Let's just grab a bite to eat. I'm pretty tired and hungry. It was a circus at the park today. I mean, a real circus was there. They had elephants, tigers, clowns... The crowd was unreal! Ringling Brothers moved some of their show from the Riverside Racetrack to Poppy's trying to drum up more business from the family crowd."

Les laughed. "That does sound crazy, so food it is. You got it," He said as he started up the car. "Is there any place you had in mind?"

"How about the Nichols Diner on 10th Street? They're open late."

"Sounds good to me," he agreed.   Pulling away from the park gate, he added, "Wasn't the fellow that owns it involved in a couple of kidnapping cases last year?"

Deloris whipped her head around. "I don't know. Tell me about it," she said, trying not to sound too eager.

"Some fellow, I can't remember his name, something like Excalibur or something, went to Poppy's amusement park with the Nichols family and was abducted from there. The newspaper said that Frank Nichols, the owner of Nichols Lunch Counter, was a go-between in the kidnapping along with a man named Brown." He paused, then added conspiratorially, "You know, Frank's brother, Gus Nichols, is a gangster who is in prison in Minnesota? Oh, Exarhos, that's the guy's name. Anyway, he escaped and told the police about the abduction. They arrested Frank in connection with the abduction of this fellow *and* the abduction of Michael Katz from Katz Pharmacy, who was kidnapped last year."

"How in the world did you remember that and why do you know so much about it?" she asked.

"I'm just smart like that. Actually, I kind of have a photographic memory and stories like that interest me, especially stories like the one in Jameson." He glanced away from the road to wink at Deloris.

At Nichols Diner, Deloris and Les found a table in the corner where they sat down. They each ordered a hamburger with a coke and sat there eating and talking until past midnight. When Les dropped her off back home, everyone was in bed except for Thelma, who had gone to work. Deloris climbed the stairs quietly and went to her room. As she started putting her things away, she realized just how tired she was, and she sat down on the bed. The next thing she knew, she was waking up still in her clothes. Looking blearily at the clock, she realized it was too early to get up, so she quickly changed into her nightgown and laid back down on her bed. But sleep didn't come, and she lay there wide awake again. So, just before her alarm went off, she arose and got ready for work.

Chapter Three

Monday, Labor Day
(September 7, 1931)

You're up early again," Thelma observed. "Are you going to make a habit of getting up early?"

Deloris yawned and stretched before reaching for the coffeepot. "I hope not. I just fell asleep early again."

Deloris left for work and caught the first bus.

This time she was prepared for the two girls who had left early the last time. She burst through the door and started talking before they could say anything.

"I'm here early, so I'm not on the clock yet. Please don't... Mrs. Miles, what are you doing here this early?" Startled, the two girls turned to look at Deloris with tears in their eyes.

Mary Virginia Miles stood in the doorway to her office with her arms crossed. Apparently, she had been watching the two girls work. When Deloris entered the room, she looked up.

"Good morning, Deloris. What are you doing here so early again?" Mary Virginia greeted her as she glanced over at the other two girls. She obviously just figured out that the girls had been clocking out early and was watching them. They looked miserable, like they had just been reprimanded. "You look chipper this morning," the older woman observed of Deloris. "What's going on with you?"

Deloris told about her job offer and Mary Virginia nodded in approval. "I have an interview tomorrow," she explained.

"I am certain they will hire you. You are a good worker,

unlike others." She again glanced over at the girls and they gave half-hearted smiles. Deloris didn't want to be held up as a comparison goal for them to hate her more, but what could she do? They got caught, plain and simple.

At five minutes to eight, Mary Virginia said, "You may leave now, but I want you two girls to clock in thirty minutes early tonight. You obviously forgot that the time clock doesn't lie."

As the girls gathered their things, Pam breezed into the room. "Are you here early again, making us look bad?" she complained. "It's a holiday! Even though the Labor Day holiday doesn't mean anything to us, since we are expected to work."

"Oh, I woke up early again," Deloris shrugged.

"I would have stayed home until it was time to go to work if I got up early. There is no way I would come here early," Pam chortled.

"I could have stayed home, but I was too excited to stay there." Deloris stood up and walked to the punch clock to put her time card in, then placed it back in the slotted card rack on the wall.

"Why are you so excited, honey child?" Joyce asked as she, Boo, and Lori walked in the door and started putting their purses in their lockers.

"I have a job interview tomorrow and now that tonight is my last night working at Poppy's, it is a gigantic relief."

"Where is the job?" Boo asked.

"Venetian Gardens over on Grand Avenue."

"Congratulations!" everyone chimed in together.

"I don't have the job yet, but the owner told me the job was mine. I'm going to see his wife for the interview. Wish me luck.

I'm a little nervous."

"Oh, you'll do just fine." Lori offered words of encouragement.

The girls took their stations, and for Deloris, the morning seemed to take forever until her switchboard lit up near the end of her shift.

"Please, we need an ambulance," a male caller said breathlessly. "My wife is having a baby, err, uh, the doctor says probably two babies and my car won't start. Hurry!"

"Sir, Sir. Calm down. What is your address?" Deloris asked.

"5505 Park Avenue. Hurry!"

Deloris plugged the wire in to call the ambulance and gave the address.

Joyce took the next call and rang for another ambulance. She repeated to the ambulance crew what she was told: "They found a body in the Missouri River. Apparently, a group of young men had been swimming a few days ago, and their friend was caught in the undercurrents. The body just came to the surface."

Boo took a call from General Hospital that she repeated back to the caller, "You need the police there, stat! You're holding a 16-year-old boy who attempted to help his brother escape police custody while he was in the hospital?"

Everyone at the switchboard could hear the caller yell, "Hurry!"

Boo continued repeating what the caller had said. "The officer assigned to watch the prisoner was knocked out. Okay, okay, we'll send the police right away."

"What does stat mean?" Boo asked as she disconnected the call and prepared to call the police downstairs.

Deloris quickly replied, "That means immediately in

Latin—rush!" For once, the Latin she had in high school came in handy.

"Oh," Boo immediately rang the front desk.

Deloris sat back and gave a sigh. "That's the last time I'll think that things are moving too slow," she thought. As she prepared to clock out at the end of her shift, she realized she hadn't told Austin about her good fortune. She grabbed her purse and headed downstairs to share her good news.

"Hey DeDe, what's up?" Austin asked as he was grabbing his hat from the coat rack and saw her walking his way. "I can't talk long. We got a call to go to the hospital to take a teenager into custody for assault. He was attempting to help his brother escape custody."

"Oh, yes, I heard that call come in. It's okay. I just wanted to tell you I have a job interview tomorrow."

"Hey, that's keen. I want to hear all about it when I get back."

"Sure, I'll see you later and tell you about it." She paused. "Oh, I also wanted to find out if you heard anything on the picnic stuff."

"Oh, it's taken care of," he said, dismissing the thought with a wave of his hand. "Okay, I'll see you later." And he was out of the office in a flash.

With everyone busy, Deloris took herself to lunch. Nance's Cafe would be a good place to relax. She hoped she might see another friend there having lunch: Dr. David Kerns. Dr. Kerns grew up in Jameson and was good friends with Deloris' oldest brother, Roy. Dr. Kerns often went to either Nance's Cafe or Woolworth's Lunch Counter with his business partner. Sometimes, Deloris met him there, and they had lunch together.

Entering the cafe, she looked around, but didn't see him,

so she sat at the counter and pulled out some paper to make notes. Just as her corned beef hash arrived, Annie Bailey, her friend, housemate and partner in adventurous activities, appeared and sat down next to her.

"What's happening, Toots?" Annie asked playfully, grabbing some of the bread Deloris was served with her hash and started buttering it.

"Oh, hey Annie," Deloris said with a smile, even as her bread disappeared. "I didn't know you'd be around here."

"Yes, I just submitted my story about a woman who confessed to committing several holdups in different areas of Kansas City and in Kansas, too. She had quite a profitable business going on!"

"I guess she would if she moved around like that. Oh, here's a tip for you: as I was leaving, Boo took a call from General Hospital about a 16-year-old who tried to help his brother escape custody and knocked the security guard out."

"Really? Oh, I'd better get over there to see if I can get more information for a story. Thanks!" She swiped one more slice of bread and disappeared as quickly as she had appeared.

Deloris spent the rest of her lunch time thinking of what she was going to say at the interview, and jotted some things down.

She went home and changed clothes to prepare for her last night at Poppy's. Typically, she didn't work on Monday nights, but because this was Labor Day, Mr. O'Brien asked everyone to work and help close the park down for the season.

Chapter Four
End of the Season

Because the weather turned chilly that Monday evening, there wasn't a large crowd—or even what you might call a crowd at all—on the last night at Poppy's. Mr. O'Brien told everyone to button everything up early, which suited Deloris just fine. Battening down the hatches for the winter, so to speak, Poppy's Paradise Park employees gave everything a final cleaning and closed up all the windows and doors. Being the end of Deloris' first summer working for Poppy's, she felt a little melancholy as she washed and put away the last soda glass. She thought about her first coworker, Paul Sullivan, and wondered how his family was doing. Unlike Paul, Virgil was always willing to do extra tasks and help. Deloris turned to Virgil, who was helping her clean up, and thanked him for being a good co-worker. Virgil looked at her quizzically, but continued with his task of putting things away in the back storeroom.

Deloris covered the glasses and dishes with tea towels and emptied the remaining ice cream mixtures that she and Virgil could either throw out or take home with them as a perk. She washed the ice cream containers while Virgil put the chairs on top of the tables and mopped the floor. Those tasks completed, they stood in the doorway and gave one last glance to make sure everything was in order before Virgil turned off the lights and closed the door. Deloris put the key in the lock and turned it one last time. As the two walked to Mr. O'Brien's office to turn in the keys and the cash bag, they saw other park employees saying their goodbyes with hugs and plans to resume their relationships the following May.

Then Deloris and Virgil walked in silence to Building C, which served as the breakroom for the staff, and on opposite ends were the lockers and dressing rooms for males and females. Inside the breakroom, Deloris turned to Virgil and told him again how nice it was to work with him and how she hated to say goodbye, but the time had come. Giving him a quick handshake, she said, "I'll see you next year."

"Yes, see you then. Thank you for helping me learn what to do and how to make the various ice cream treats," he said with a look of admiration on his face.

"That's okay. Someone once taught me learn how to make them when I first started," Deloris said with a smile, remembering her first day at the soda fountain and how she didn't know how to make a strawberry sundae.

She then turned and walked to the women's locker room. Inside the room, Deloris found her friends Stella and Trudie just finishing up changing their clothes.

"Hey, Deloris, do you want to go out on the town and trip the light fantastic with us tonight?" Stella offered.

"I'd love to go, but I have a date with Leon tonight and work tomorrow," Deloris explained as she reached for her street clothes.

"How about tomorrow night?"

"Sorry, I have a date with Les tomorrow tonight, but I really do want to go out with you two. Raincheck?"

"Wait, you've got another boyfriend? Who is Les? What does Leon think about that? Where did you meet this new guy?"

Deloris laughed and put up her hands. "Hold on, one at a time. I met Les up in Jameson, but he is from Independence, and Leon doesn't know about Les and Les doesn't know about Leon and neither needs to know about the other," she said with a sly smile.

"You're dating *two* guys?" Stella almost yelled.

"Shush."

"How do you keep them all straight?" Trudie said, shaking her head in disbelief.

"I only have two boys I am dating. It's not that hard. I dated three boys at the same time when I was in high school," Deloris retorted with a wink. "But in a small town, I had to be careful. They were all from other towns nearby." The girls giggled as they grabbed their coats and headscarves.

Stella stopped and interrupted, "Okay, so you can't go tonight or tomorrow night. You owe us the details about this Les person. How about we get together on Wednesday or Thursday night? Or do you have a date with another guy on one of those nights?"

"No. Don't be silly. I'm free either night."

Deloris finished changing her clothes, said goodbye to her friends, as they all exited Poppy's for the last time until the following spring. Outside the entrance, she found Leon Iraklidis sitting in his beige with brown trim 1930 Model A Sports Coupe Convertible Chevrolet Cabriolet, waiting for her. Deloris met Leon when she first started working at the soda fountain. He was the one who helped her learn the other different ice cream concoctions. Then asked her out.

"Hi there. Hop in." Once she settled into the seat, Leon continued, "Where shall we go?"

"I don't really care. I'm just hungry," she said, smiling sweetly at him as she climbed into his car. "Thank you for picking me up, by the way. Last time until next year."

"It's okay. I'm happy to get to spend some time with you. How about that new restaurant called the Aida Cafe? They have Italian and American food and a six-piece band with dancing from 8 p.m. to 2 a.m."

"Not sure I can make it until 2 a.m. dancing," Deloris admitted. "I am a little punchy, and I have work tomorrow at the switchboard, but the food sounds good to me. One thing about Kansas City, it has a lot of restaurants to choose from and a cornucopia of food choices."

As they drove, Deloris told him about the job offer from Mr. Binaggio.

Leon glanced over at her, concerned. "Is he connected to the mob? You need to be careful of that, you know."

"I don't know." She cocked her head thoughtfully. "He might be, but he was very nice."

"Gangsters can be very nice. If you show them respect, they show you respect. Just be aware," he said with a concerned look on his face.

"How do you know that?" she asked suspiciously.

"That's what I've heard. Don't worry, I'm not with the mob," he laughed.

"Don't worry. I can take care of myself, but I will be careful," she replied, a little annoyed at him taking a fatherly tone with her.

Chapter Five

The Interview

Tuesday morning, Deloris wore her best hat and dress to work and endured teasing from her coworkers at the switchboard for dressing so fancy.

"Look at you. What are you all gussied up for?" Joyce asked.

"Today is my interview for the new job," Deloris reminded her.

"Oh, that's right. Well, good luck," Joyce offered.

When her shift ended, Deloris figured that if she left then for the Venetian Gardens Italian Restaurant, she'd be almost two hours early. So, she went downstairs to see if Austin wanted to go to lunch, but he was out on a call and wouldn't be back for a while. Lori, who also just got off work, was at the entrance to the police station when Deloris exited the building.

"Are you waiting for a bus?" Deloris asked.

"Yes, but it seems to be late," Lori responded, looking at her watch.

"Do you need to go somewhere right away? Would you like to go to lunch with me?" Deloris offered.

"I was just thinking about lunch myself. Sure, where shall we go?"

"I thought I would go to Engleman's Cafeteria, because it's

close to Venetian Gardens, where I have the interview."

"Sounds good to me," Lori agreed. "I've got a little time."

As they arrived and settled at a table, Deloris asked, "So, tell me about yourself? We've never really had time to talk and get to know each other."

Deloris learned Lori was from Blue Springs, a suburb of Kansas City, and caught the bus to the city for her shifts at the switchboard. She grew up on a farm, but was thinking about moving to the city to be closer to work. Her second job was working as a waitress, too. The girls found they had a lot in common and vowed to have lunch again in the future. Lori had to leave at one-thirty, but it wasn't time for Deloris to leave yet.

When twenty minutes to two finally arrived, Deloris left Engelman's and walked the three blocks to the Venetian Gardens Restaurant. It was a small, red brick building midway on the block, wedged between two buildings: the building on the south advertised the latest in soda pop and other non-alcoholic beverages, while the other building was a shop for all kinds of repairs, from toasters to motor car tires. A large parking lot was the next lot north.

Deloris opened the Venetian Gardens door under an arched trellis covered in grapevines, and was immediately hit with the smell of garlic, onions, and tomatoes, but unfortunately stale cigarette smoke, too, which ruined the delectable aroma from the food. The restaurant was dark, as large windows on either side of the door had curtains pulled closed, requiring lights to be on inside. The thick grapevines also covered the windows, contributing to the dimly lit interior.

She waited for her eyes to adjust to the darker interior before walking forward. To the left was a long counter that formerly served as a bar to offer all kinds of libations, but today, with Prohibition still enforced, it only served as a counter for single patrons to sit at and eat. Tables and chairs were placed all about the main room, with one big table at the front for a large group and smaller tables around and behind it. In the back of the room, opposite from the front door, was a door to the kitchen, and just to the right was a spot for a small band to set up.

A short, round man behind the counter spoke up with a raspy voice, "What can I do for you, little lady?" His face was pockmarked, Deloris assumed from a severe case of acne as a teenager. His brown hair, dusted with silver around his ears, was thin on top, and she felt as if his eyes drilled holes through to her very soul.

Deloris gulped. "I, I'm here to see, see C-C-Connie," she stammered, as she sometimes still did when she was nervous. "Nino sent me."

"Wait here," he commanded. "I'll get Connie."

After almost five minutes, Connie appeared from the back doorway. She was a gorgeous woman, about 40–50 years old, wearing a stylish dress, long pearls, and black high heels. Her long brown and gray hair was pulled up into a bun. Her makeup was impeccable, with her crimson lips and fingernails painted to match. She looked more like a fashion model than a restaurant manager.

In a melodious contralto voice, she said, "Hello," as she extended a hand. "I understand Nino sent you."

"Ye-yes, he did," Deloris replied. "He-he came to see me at

P-P-Poppy's and told me he had a j-job for me and that I sh-should come see you."

She glanced over at the fellow behind the counter, who was watching her closely and contributed to her nervousness. Something about the Venetian Gardens felt ominous, and that man, especially, gave her a feeling that he might belong to the Italian Mafia. She could easily see him involved in illegal activity.

She continued, "You may know, P-P-Poppy's is closed and I need a j-job for the winter and..."

Deloris stopped because she realized she was now running her words together and needed to slow down. Taking a deep breath, she looked into Connie's kind eyes and waited a minute to organize in her mind what she was going to say next, then continued,

"Mr. Binaggio told me you might have a job opening here and that I should come talk with you."

"Yes, dear," Connie smiled and motioned to a seat at a nearby table. The man at the counter then turned and started busily cleaning glasses and watching the front door. "Deloris, is it? Is that the name we should call you?"

"Yes, ma'am."

"Nino told me a little about you and that you would be coming today." Connie took a seat gracefully.

"Yes, ma'am," Deloris said as she sat down across from her. "I rarely stutter. I'm just a little nervous."

"You needn't be nervous. We're all friends here. Isn't that right, Sal?"

Sal had his back to them, but turned his head and nodded in agreement, then continued drying the glass in his hand.

"You come highly recommended, Deloris. Nino really likes what he heard about your work ethic. You can relax. Once you are in, you will be taken care of and won't need to look for work again," she said with a wink.

She continued, "As you know, my name is Connie. Constantina, really, but please call me Connie. I am Nino's wife. Over there is Nino's brother, Sal." Facing them now, he raised the glass in his hand to signify a hello toast. "Why don't you tell me a little about yourself?"

Feeling a little more at ease, Deloris began, "Well, I grew up in north Missouri on a small farm. I have two brothers and a sister. I graduated in May at the age of eighteen and I will be nineteen later this month. I was held back in first grade because of the Spanish Flu. I work, rather, I worked at Poppy's Paradise Park on weekends, until yesterday, as you know. I started working there the last of May. During the week, in the mornings only, I work at a switchboard. I mean, I answer a phone at the, uh, egg factory. I worked on a switchboard in my hometown before I graduated, so I often mess that up."

Austin had warned Deloris when she first went to work at the Kansas City Police Department to be careful who she told about working there. Corruption could be found at all levels, and she shouldn't trust anyone but her closest friends with that information. Although she used it to her advantage when she was investigating the murder up in Jameson, she never even told her boss at Poppy's Paradise Park about working at the police department and he never asked where she worked in the mornings. Besides, when she started her job at Poppy's, she *was* working at the egg factory and never told Mr. O'Brien anything different when she lost that job. So, Deloris thought that giving the egg factory would be a safe job to give to Connie, since it was only a half lie. She had worked there, just not now and not answering the phone. If they checked, her hiring paperwork would be there. Although it was a safe bet, no one would follow up to check on her employment there, anyway.

"So, you've never worked in a restaurant?"

"No, the closest to it was working at the soda fountain a t Poppy's."

"Okay, Miss Markham. We can train you with what you need to know. It looks like you will be a good fit here. Show up Friday at 4 p.m. and we'll get you started. Pay is $7 a day, plus tips. Here is a menu. Study it so you know what we serve."

"Oh, Mr. Binaggio said that it would be $27 a week, $9 a day, plus tips."

"That is true for someone experienced, but we will need to train you first, then it can go up from there," Connie explained.

Doris was disappointed, but said, "I understand."

"Follow me." Connie stood and led Deloris through the kitchen door and to her office in the back right of the kitchen. She went to her desk, sat down, and shuffled around in her desk drawers. After a few moments, she said, "I need you to fill out the hiring paperwork. I would have you fill it out today, but it looks like I need to get some copies made. Come in tomorrow about this time and you can fill them out then. Is that okay with you?"

"Oh, yes."

"Please be here on Friday by 4 o'clock for us to walk you through everything you need to know the first night." With that, Connie arose from her chair and offered Deloris a handshake.

Deloris stepped forward and shook her hand. "Thank you very much for the job, Mrs. Binaggio." Connie cocked her head at Deloris and Deloris corrected herself. "Connie, I mean. I'll see you tomorrow and then again Friday at 4 p.m."

Deloris was excited to have a job, although she was pretty sure they had gangster connections. She was fairly certain she saw a Colt Detective Special gun, also known as a snub-nose 38, in Connie's desk drawer. How did she know what it was? Austin showed her the one he had and told her all about it. Then Sal was the epitome of every gangster she had seen in the movies. He looked sinister, like he would have no qualms putting a bullet in someone's head. She tried not to focus on that. A job is a job, she thought. Even though she wasn't comfortable with the atmosphere, she liked to make money. She was disappointed that the pay wasn't more, but she would work hard to get that extra two dollars a day. She promised she would get to know Sal better and make him a friend. It couldn't hurt having someone that scary as a friend to protect you when the Austin wasn't around. On the bus ride home, she studied the menu and felt she had a pretty good grasp of it.

Chapter Six

A Job is a Job

Deloris went home elated that she had a job to start Friday. She convinced herself, it was just an Italian restaurant, and she was being unfair to categorize Sal, Connie, and Nino. When she got home, she found Thelma up early from her rest so that she could start supper and prepare to go to work at the egg factory. She found Annie at home, too, helping Thelma by shucking corn for some corn on the cob.

"Did you get a story out of the 16-year-old at the hospital?" she asked.

"I sure did. Check out the paper tomorrow," Annie said with a big smile.

"I am thrilled for you. I can't wait to read it."

"Hey DeDe, how'd the job interview go?" Thelma asked as she came from the kitchen.

"I start Friday," Deloris said with a smile.

"That's great. Do you want to help me get supper ready?" Thelma asked

"Why not?" Deloris followed her into the kitchen, donned an apron, and went to work on peeling potatoes. Then Annie put the corn in a pan of water she had on the stove. Gracie came home and started setting the table with Leota when she came downstairs. They propped the kitchen door open so that everyone could take part in the "what's new" conversations. They were always Deloris' favorite part of the day.

"So, tell me about this new job," Thelma inquired.

Gracie came to the door and said, "Yes, tell us *all* about it."

"Well, it's at the Venetian Gardens down on Grand. It is an Italian restaurant managed by Connie Binaggio, who is married to the owner, Nino Binaggio. Oh, and then there is Sal, the guy who works behind the counter." With a small shudder she continued, "He kind of scares me with the way he looked at me, kind of like he saw right through me. The whole place is kind of dark and ominous, but hey it is a job, and I can brighten it up," Deloris said, with an optimistic smile.

"If anyone can brighten a place up, it is you, DeDe," Gracie said with a wink. After that comment, Leota mumbled something and left the dining room.

Suddenly, Deloris dropped the potato peeler. "I almost forgot. I won't be eating supper tonight. I need to go upstairs and get ready for my date!"

Deloris breezed through the living room, ignoring Leota's scowl. When Deloris came back downstairs, she answered the knock at the door. It was Les Wells.

"Hello, Deloris," Les said with glad eyes and a wide grin on his face. "You look like a knockout."

"Hi there," Deloris responded with a coy grin on her face.

"Are you ready to howl at the night?"

"I am. I'll see you later, folks," she said as she waved goodbye to Thelma, Gracie, and Annie, who were standing in the dining room watching with their mouths open.

"Have fun. Don't stay out too late." Annie replied, grinning and beating Thelma to saying it.

Deloris groaned, shaking her head, and closed the door.

The next day, at the end of her shift, Deloris went down to Austin's desk. "Are you free for lunch today?"

He looked up from his usual pile of paperwork. "Sure. Let me put these files away and I'll be right with you."

A few minutes later, they settled into a table at Woolworth's. "How are you doing?" Austin asked. "Are you feeling better?"

"I'm doing okay, now that I have a job and you took care of my other worries. You did take care of them, didn't you?" She smiled sweetly at him in appreciation.

"Yeah, yeah. All is well there. So, tell me about your new job again?"

Before she could answer, two guys at the lunch counter started arguing somewhat loudly, and it looked like they were about to take a swing at each other. Austin jumped up and pulled them apart, de-escalating the situation quickly.

Holding firmly to an arm of each man, Austin apologized. "Sorry DeDe. It looks like these two thugs just earned a ride to the police station. I'll see you later. Okay?"

"Of course. It looks like you have your hands full anyway," she said with a smirk, since she intended it to be a pun. "Do you want to come by the house later?"

One guy started squirming and Austin held his arm tighter. "That'd be great," he replied as he dragged the two out of the door.

Alone with her thoughts, Deloris did some people watching—one of her favorite hobbies. In her mind, she worked out a whole scenario for each person's life. She gave them a name and decided what they did for a living and what kind of person they were, all from just observing them.

When one-thirty arrived, Deloris left Woolworths and started walking down Main to Eighth Street. Woolworth's was a little farther away from the restaurant than Engleman's, but only a few blocks. Luckily, it was a beautiful September day, not too cool and not too hot. Just right for a walk.

Entering the Venetian Gardens, Deloris noticed Sal was nowhere to be seen, but Connie came walking up to the door and greeted her.

"I came to fill out the paperwork," Deloris said.

"Oh yes, follow me." Connie led her to her office.

"Where's Sal?"

"Oh, he's gone to collect an order and will be back? Why?"

"Well, to be honest, he scares me. I thought I would try to be friends with him and get over that feeling."

Connie laughed and said, "He's really a big teddy bear, but don't tell him I said that or he'll become angry like a bull in a china closet. You'd be surprised what kind of riff-raff we get in here from time to time, and he needs to be tough to keep everyone in line."

Sitting at her desk, Connie reached into her desk drawer, pushed the gun aside, and produced two sheets of paper.

"Here you go. Fill these out, please." She left the room while Deloris filled them out and came back five minutes later. "All done?"

"Yes, ma'am." She stood up and handed Connie the papers.

"Okay, we will see you here on Friday."

"You said to be here at 4 o'clock, correct?"

"That's correct."

Later that afternoon, Deloris and Gracie were home getting the evening meal started when Thelma got up and started mixing up a cake. Austin came sauntering into the kitchen. "What are all of you bumping gums about?"

"What?" Thelma asked while Deloris answered.

"We were talking about my new job."

"Oh yeah. How'd your interview go? Where was it again?"

"Well, I start on Friday and it is at the Venetian Gardens Restaurant on Grand Boulevard."

"Venetian Gardens? Something sounds familiar about that name. Tell me all about it," Austin said with a genuine interest as he sat down and pulled out his notepad and wrote something in it.

"Nino Binaggio told me to talk with his wife, Connie Binaggio at her restaurant about a job. So, I met with her yesterday and she offered me the job. Nino's brother, Sal Binaggio, works there too. He looks like a big mean guy and scares me, but I've decided to be friendly toward him and maybe he'll reciprocate."

Austin wrote several things on his notepad. When Deloris

noticed, she asked, "What are you doing?"

"Oh, I just thought that I'd do a little checking on Sal and Nino."

"Don't jinx my new job," Deloris protested.

"I won't, but you can't be too careful these days."

"Okay, but I did what you said, and I didn't tell anyone that I work at the police station."

Austin interrupted with a raised eyebrow, "At the *switchboard*?"

"Yes, yes, at the switchboard," Deloris said, waving her hand dismissively. She described Connie, Nino, and Sal to him. He listened intently and wrote more things down in his notepad.

"Do you want me to look into Sal and his background?"

"You don't need to do that. I'll be fine. Mr. and Mrs. Binaggio are nice people. I'm sure they'll I'll be fine to work for."

"Okay, but I'll still just look them up," Austin said. "So, what's for supper? I mean, uh…"

Laughingly, Thelma responded, "Do you want to stay for supper?"

"It sure smells good. Okay, you twisted my arm. I'll stay," he said with a satisfied grin.

Annie and Leota arrived in the dining room from different areas of the house and joined Gracie, Thelma, and Deloris in the meal preparations. One began setting the table, another retrieved the glasses from the china closet, and Gracie started placing napkins and silverware on the table. Deloris went upstairs to get Thelma's daughters ready for supper.

Watching the crew of helpers, Austin asked, "Hey Thelma, did you ever rent the room that belonged to Juanita?" Juanita was a former boarder who had rented the room at the back that Thelma had remodeled from a back porch.

Thelma grimaced at her name. "Not yet. Why? Do you have someone in mind?"

"Big Jim's girlfriend, Edith Wellington, is looking for a place now. You may have heard last week that there was a gangland shooting right outside the entryway doors of the Mosby Apartments at 511 West 11th Street? They killed three gangsters and wounded two more. On top of that, the week before, some hoodlums stole three cars on that block, and a month ago, a woman on the first floor came home just in time to see a man walk out the back of her building with his arms full of food. When she went into her kitchen, she found the food came from her pantry and icebox. Edith lives there and has been talking about moving for a while, but after the shooting she doesn't feel safe there anymore and wants out sooner rather than later."

"Have her come by tomorrow around one o'clock and I'll show her the room."

"I wanted to rent that room," Leota complained.

"Yes, dear, I know, but I need you on the top floor with the girls so that you can help with them. Besides, the rent for that room is more than what you can afford."

"I know." Leota mumbled as she sat down hard upon the dining room chair, glowering at Thelma and giving a mean look to Deloris, for some reason.

Chapter Seven

The New Boarder

Edith Wellington arrived at Thelma's that Thursday afternoon before Thelma laid down for her afternoon nap. Deloris, who met her once before at Big Jim's desk, answered the door, "Well, hello. Come on in."

"Thank you. I've come to talk with Thelma," Edith said as Deloris invited her inside.

"Yes, I'll ..." before Deloris could say any more Thelma answered, coming from the kitchen, "That's me. You must be Edith." She extended her hand to Edith.

"I am, she," Edith replied with a warm, friendly smile. She was about twenty-five years old with golden brown hair, blue eyes, a cute oval face, and dimples. She had the aura of a teacher, though, that with one look, an errant student would immediately stop what they were doing. This was very helpful in a chemistry lab where one wrong ingredient could blow up in the student's face.

Thelma gestured for Edith to take a seat in the living room and asked, "Can I get you a glass of iced tea or coffee?"

"A coffee would be nice," the younger woman said as she placed her purse and gloves on the sofa next to her.

Deloris jumped in and offered, "I'll get it. You two sit down and relax." As she turned to go into the kitchen, Deloris stopped to ask, "Do you want cream and sugar?"

"Yes, please, to both." Turning to Thelma, she continued, "You have a nice home here."

"Thank you. I was able to buy it with the help of my former in-laws," Thelma explained.

"Oh, that is nice to have that kind of relationship with your former in-laws. How long have you lived here?" Edith asked.

"I've lived her almost five years," Thelma replied.

Shortly thereafter, Deloris returned with the drinks and set them on the coffee table in front of the sofa. She offered a cup of coffee to Edith and got one for herself before sitting down in the overstuffed chair next to Thelma's rocking chair and facing Edith.

Thelma sat there for just a second, looking at Edith, when she said, "Now, tell me about yourself."

"Well, I grew up in Independence, Missouri, and graduated from William Chrisman High School," she began. "I then went to school at Central Missouri State Teacher's College in Warrensburg where I received my degree in science. I recently started teaching chemistry at the University of Kansas City and formerly taught at the Kansas City Junior College. I've been here in the city for three years. My boyfriend is Jim Anderson, and he works with Austin Martin, whom I believe you know."

"Yes, I do. In fact, Austin recommended you to me."

"Yes, well, that is about all I know to tell you about me," Edith said with a shrug and a small smile that showed dimples. "Except I am generally quiet and pay my rent on time."

Deloris broke in, "Austin said that there was a shooting in front of your apartment building?"

Thelma, wincing, said, "We don't need to talk about that now, Deloris."

"Oh, I don't mind," Edith answered. "But yes, it was horrible. Bodies were everywhere! The police had the entrance taped off and wouldn't allow anyone in or out. I was trapped in my apartment until Jim came up to escort me out the back door."

"That must have been a terrible experience," Deloris commiserated.

"I think you will find everything here less hectic," Thelma stated, trying to steer the conversation back to a less disturbing topic.

"Sounds good to me," Edith said, her smile returning.

"Let me show you the room. It isn't much, but I had it converted from a back porch." After they walked through to the back of the house, Thelma continued, "I had extra insulation added, heavy curtains that can be pulled back in the summer, and a wood stove to ensure that it would be warm in the winter. It is also the coolest room in the house at night when you open up all the windows on three sides for cross ventilation. As you see, there is a bed, dresser and wardrobe." She pointed to one corner. "I did have my wringer washing machine over there, but I moved it to the basement where it can be rolled out in the summer or left there to use in the winter. I'll show it to you later if you decide to move in."

"Oh yes. I'll take it," Edith eagerly replied.

"Okay, then," Thelma agreed. "I don't allow men in the house after 11 p.m. and the doors are locked at midnight. Everyone is expected to help get the meals on the table or wash the dishes and clean up. Rent is $3 a week."

"Sounds good to me. When can I move in?"

"As soon as you like. It is available now."

"Okay, I'll be here to move in tomorrow."

"I'd appreciate it if you would wait to move in after I get home from my job at the diner and before I take my nap, since my room is near yours. I should be home by two in the afternoon, since I don't work at the egg factory tomorrow night. I'll be taking a late nap." She reached into her dress pocket and pulled out two keys to hand to Edith. "Here is your key to the back door in your room and a key to the front door."

Taking them with a small nod, Edith said gratefully, "Thank you. I'll see you tomorrow then."

The next day, Deloris headed out for lunch after her shift at the switchboard, stopping downstairs to see if Austin and Big Jim wanted to join her. Walking up to the front desk, she greeted the Desk Sergeant, Ted Cox.

"Hey Ted, how are you today?"

"Hello, Deloris. I suppose you are here to see Austin."

"I was hoping to catch him and go to lunch."

"Go ahead, have a seat at his desk. He's in the captain's office, but should be out directly," Sergeant Cox offered.

"Thank you."

When Austin came out of the captain's office a few minutes later, he greeted her, "Hey DeDe, how's tricks?"

"Just wondering if you are free for lunch?"

"Sure, what have you got in mind?" he said as he grabbed his hat.

"How about going to the Forum Cafeteria?" Deloris suggested.

"Sounds good to me. Today, they have a 21-cent lunch special with meatloaf, buttered carrots, corn muffin and angel food cake," Austin said, licking his lips.

"Forum Cafeteria it is then."

As they sat down to eat, Deloris asked, "Did you find anything out yet about the Binaggios?"

"No, sorry. I've been too busy to do that, but I will soon."

After lunch, Deloris went home to rest and then get ready for her new job. She was in the dining room reading the paper before she had to leave for work when Edith and Big Jim arrived.

"Well, hello again. Oh, that's right. You are moving in today, aren't you?" she said as she opened the door, eyeing the box Big Jim was carrying and the bags Edith had in tow.

"Yes, that is what Thelma and I agreed to yesterday."

"Welcome to our humble abode," Deloris said, stepping back to let them into the house. "You will be a vast improvement over the last tenant we had in there. Big Jim can tell you about her."

Edith looked at Big Jim curiously and he said, "I'll tell you all about it later." They then resumed carrying her belongings into the back bedroom. Thelma came out of her room and Edith said, "I hope we didn't wake you."

"Oh no, I was awake."

After he carried in the last box, Jim turned to say goodbye.

"Do you want to stay for supper, Jim?" Thelma offered. "We always have plenty."

"How can I refuse a home-cooked meal by Thelma Webb?" he said with a twinkle in his eye. Big Jim took a seat at the dining room table and Edith came out of the room to join him, Deloris, and Thelma.

Annie was the first of the boarders to arrive home from work. She was a little earlier than usual. "Hello," she said as she walked over to Edith and extended her hand. "I'm Annie Bailey, and you are?"

"I'm Edith Wellington. The new boarder."

"Oh, so, you are moving into the back room?"

"Yes, I just moved in."

"You'll like it. It is one of the quietest rooms in the entire house and you'll like it here. We are like one big, happy family," Annie said warmly.

"That's good to know," Edith said as her dimples reappeared.

Just then, Leota, with Thelma's daughters, walked in the door to face the lively chatter and chaos. Startled, Leota looked at the group sitting at the table, mumbled something, and retreated up the stairs to her room. The girls seemed to take no notice and resumed a game of jacks that they played the night before in a corner of the living room.

Annie turned to Edith and said with a wink, "Well, most of us are like one big happy family."

"What do you do, Annie?" Edith asked.

"I am a reporter for *The Kansas City Post* newspaper."

"Oh, really? That must be exciting."

"It can be," Annie said with a smile. "Following Deloris around has been the most exciting and productive."

Deloris stuck her tongue out at Annie and they laughed.

When Gracie arrived home, she immediately ran up to her room to put her books and purse away before hurrying back downstairs to join the group. As she entered the dining room, she started talking, "Guess what we did in school today?" but stopped suddenly. "Miss Wellington, what are you doing here?"

When Gracie started school a week ago, she had been eager to tell her roommates about the new chemistry teacher who was a woman. Women teaching in higher education was a rarity, especially in a science class, and Miss Wellington became an inspiration for all of Gracie's female classmates. They all admired her.

Startled, Edith looked up to see one of her new chemistry pupils looking back at her in shock. "Hello, Miss Burnett. I didn't know that you lived here." Edith looked at Big Jim with a look of disbelief and distress.

"Oh, you must be Gracie's new science teacher that we've heard so much about," Deloris commented, highlighting the reason for Gracie's discomfort.

"I don't think that I should stay here, Thelma. My apologies," Edith said as she rose from her seat.

"Don't be silly. I'm sure that we can work something out," Thelma offered. "I really want you for a tenant. Good tenants are hard to find these days."

Edith shook her head. "I will still look to see if I can find another place. It won't be easy, but I am certain I will find one."

"Oh Miss Wellington, I am only in chemistry for one semester. We only have to worry about this for a couple of months and then it won't be an issue," Gracie urged.

Edith sighed. "I suppose I wouldn't find a place for a month or two, anyway. You have a point. Can we dispense with formalities while we are here then? You may call me Edith."

"Okay, Edith, and please call me Gracie. I am very happy you will live here," Gracie said excitedly.

"I don't want the other students to know that we are both living here," Edith said as she sat back down. "I don't want them to think that I will favor you, so we mustn't let others know about this."

"I won't tell anyone; besides the people I am closest to are here and already know," she said with a wink. "I won't even bother you when I have a question until we are in class."

"Good. I think that is wise."

Leota came down the stairs, and her eyes were red as if she had been crying.

The first to notice, Deloris asked, "Are you okay?"

"I'm fine," Leota answered rather abruptly, crossing her arms over her chest. Then she glared at Edith and Big Jim.

"Oh, Leota Jones, this is Edith Wellington and her boyfriend, Jim Anderson. Edith is taking the room at the back," Deloris announced.

"Hello," Leota said, as her expression softening a bit, and then fixed herself a glass of tea before taking a seat at the end of the dining room table.

"So, tell me about yourself Leota, what do you do, besides babysit the girls here?" Edith asked, trying to smooth out the awkwardness.

Caught off-guard that anyone would talk to her, Leota almost choked on the tea. She wasn't accustomed to people noticing her. When she regained her composure, she replied, "I am a maid at the President Hotel."

"Where are you from?"

"Kansas City."

"Where did you go to school?"

"Westport."

"I see." When Leota clearly wasn't going to elaborate, Edith went on, "And what about you, Gracie? I don't really know about you outside of school."

"I'm from Sedalia, Missouri, and I work at the Kansas City Police Department switchboard on weekends. I want to become a coroner, like Deloris' friend Carolyn, and that is why I am in school."

"Good for you," Edith said, nodding her head in approval.

Big Jim interrupted, "Carolyn is the assistant coroner."

"One day, maybe she will be the coroner," Gracie added.

Deloris looked around the table and could see that Edith was a pleasant addition to their little group. She hoped that Edith would be staying and not find another place to stay. Glancing at her watch, she jumped up and gave her apologies for leaving, and ran out the door.

Chapter Eight
Venetian Gardens

Deloris caught a bus and headed to the Venetian Gardens to start her first shift. She took another glance at the menu before the bus arrived at the Venetian Gardens. Inside the restaurant, the smell of oregano, onions, and garlic greeted her again. Sal was behind the bar again, wiping it down.

"Hello Sal. How are you? Is Connie here?"

"In the back," he said, tossing his head in that direction. Sal was obviously a man of few words, but his intense gaze spoke volumes. But this time, he mustered a small smile.

"Connie must have told him what I said," Deloris thought. He still made her nervous, but she again vowed to get to know him better, to hopefully get over it. She walked rigidly to the kitchen door, glancing back at Sal, who was watching her. A chill went up her spine, and she quickly pushed opened the door, stepping toward the source of the delicious smells. Connie was talking to the cook, a woman who was obviously upset about something. Connie looked up and saw Deloris.

"Deloris, you're a little early."

"I know. It is one of my habits to arrive early. Oh, here is the menu back."

"Well, there is nothing wrong with that habit," Connie said with a smile as she took the menu from Deloris. "Oh, these are our cooks. This is Franny. Her name is really Francesca

Casciola, but she prefers to be called Franny, and over there is her sister, Olivia Fontana, and Franny's son, Enzo Casciola."

"How do you do?" Deloris reached out her hand to shake Franny's, but Franny showed her hands were covered with flour from making homemade spaghetti, so Deloris just waved. Meatballs were bobbing up and down in a bubbling tomato sauce cooking on the stove. Olivia was rolling more meatballs in olive oil and placing them on a pan to go in the oven. Enzo was cutting onions and just waved too.

"Welcome to our piece of heaven. Sorry, this is our busy time and we really don't have time to talk," Franny said apologetically. "We're getting food ready for tonight and tomorrow night."

"I understand; it smells great. Nice to meet you."

Another girl with brown hair pulled back in a bun, wearing glasses and no makeup, came rushing into the kitchen and started back to the office, but Connie stopped her.

"Lilly, hey. This is Deloris. I just hired her and she'll be working with you tonight."

"Thank God," was Lilly's reply. "We need another person. Hi, I'm Lilly. Lilly Ross. I'll help you as much as I can." She extended her hand to shake.

Reaching out her own hand, Deloris said, "Thank you. Nice to meet you."

"Likewise," Lilly said, and hurried off to put her things in the office.

"Okay, let's get you set up," Connie said as she ushered Deloris into her office and pointed to two lockers off to the side. "This is where you can put your purse and coat." Deloris noticed that both lockers had broken locks and looked at Connie.

Seeing the quizzical look on Deloris's face, Connie added, "Oh, there's no need to lock them. I lock the office when I'm not in here and I can assure you, I won't bother your things." She went to a cupboard and pulled out a folded apron and handed it to Deloris. Then she handed her a pad of paper to write orders upon and a pencil. "There, you should be all set."

"How do I record my time?"

"You can just write it down on this sheet of paper." Connie pointed at a sheet of paper on the corner of her desk. "Come, let me walk you around the restaurant so that you are familiar with where we have everything."

"Okay," Deloris said, feeling a little unsure. With everything different and a new organizational arrangement than at her previous employment, she wondered how this would work out, but at least she had Lilly to ask.

At five o'clock, Connie unlocked the door and the first customers arrived. Connie greeted them like old friends, showing them to a table on the edge of the room, and handing them a menu. Lilly took their order, while Deloris observed.

Then another couple arrived, and Connie took them to a table on the opposite side from the first couple. She looked at Deloris to give her the cue that she was to come take their order and Lilly followed to observe her.

Three men walked in and Connie showed them to the big table at the front of the restaurant that had a reserved sign on it. Soon, they were joined by four more men, and a brotherhood of smoking, drinking, and laughing ensued. Lilly and Deloris, in tandem, took their orders and served the table.

"Hello, may I get you something to drink?" Deloris asked as she put a small loaf of bread, along with a small bowl of olive oil sprinkled with herbal spices, in front of a couple seated next to the big table.

The man looked up and smiled. "You're new here, aren't you?"

"Yes, this is my first day, I mean, night."

The woman just sat there, sizing Deloris up and scowling. "Her husband must like to flirt, much to her dismay," Deloris thought.

"Well, doll," he continued, oblivious. "I'll have a Chianti, and my wife here will have a nice Pinot Grigio."

"Coming right up, sir. Oh, uh, I we don't have any alcohol, you know."

"Oh, yes. Just bring us some of Sal's special-blend of coffee."

Deloris went to the bar to tell Sal about the wine order. He said, "I'll take care of it."

He returned a short time later with two coffee cups full of the special coffee and placed them in front of the couple. Deloris stood slightly behind him. When he turned and left, she stepped forward.

"What would you like to order?" Deloris asked, with pad and pencil poised to write.

The man handed her the menu. "I'll have a veal parmigiano with a side of spaghetti and she'll have spaghetti and meatballs. We'll both have antipasto first."

Deloris jotted that down and hurried to the window between the kitchen and the dining area to stick the order on a spindle sitting there on the windowsill. She then went into the kitchen to where the salad fixings were situated. Olivia instructed her how much salad, or antipasto as the menu called it, to place on the salad plates and where to find the vinegar and oil cruets. Deloris took the antipasto to the customers and, as she was placing the plate in front of the man, she felt a pinch on her behind. She jumped and straightened quickly, noticing that he had a big smile on his face. His wife's glare became more intense.

Franny saved Deloris from that moment of unpleasantness when she rang a bell near the spindle and yelled "Order up!" Deloris left to collect the order, which she served to another couple. Then, when that couple's order was ready, she was careful how she served them, standing at the side of the table, just out of the man's reach. She gathered both of their salad plates and then stretched across the table to place his plate in front of him.

Later, she cornered Lilly in the kitchen and told her what had happened.

"Oh, honey, that's a form of flattery. Italian men pinch beautiful women on the rump as a compliment! It is called *pacca sul sedere*."

"Well, I'm not accustomed to that form of flattery," Deloris said, annoyed.

"You'll get used to it," Lilly said with a shrug.

As Deloris went back into the dining room, a single man walked in and Connie sat him at a table in the back. He immediately started reading the newspaper he brought with him. Deloris walked up to his table and asked what she could get for him.

"Just a coffee for now," he said without looking up from the newspaper he was hiding behind.

"Did you want the special blend coffee?"

"What? No, just regular," he said, still not looking at Deloris.

After she brought him the coffee, an order was up, so she left to get it and serve it to another table. She stopped at a different table and took their order. On her way to the kitchen, she stopped at the back table where the man was sitting. Grabbing a coffee pot from a serving table nearby, she held it up and said, "Would you like for me to freshen that up for you?"

The man finally moved his newspaper and looked up at Deloris, who captivated him instantly.

"Sure, doll. I haven't seen you here before," he said as he pushed his coffee cup closer to her, gazing into her eyes. "Did you just step out of my dreams? Am I dreaming?"

Deloris smiled cautiously.

"I haven't seen you here before. What's your story?" he asked.

"Tonight is my first night," she answered as she refilled his coffee. "Do you want to order?"

"Naw, sweetheart. I just want to get lost in your eyes. You're an angel. Am I dead? Did I die and somehow am in heaven?"

He reached for her hand, but she quickly avoided his grasp, laughing, "Okay, you are very much alive and this isn't heaven."

Each time she came to his table to refill his coffee, he made continued attempts to pick Deloris up. He asked her to go with him to the Pla-mor and she declined. Deloris knew his type. He never saw a woman he didn't like. Deloris just smiled and shook her head. She found Lilly in the kitchen and asked her who the man was reading the newspaper at the back table.

"Oh, Sam? He's a regular here, always sits at the back and watches people. Lilly rolled her eyes. I don't know why or what he does for a living. I just know that he is a big flirt."

"You can say that again. He must be a big flirt. He wants me to go to the Pla-Mor with him."

When Deloris walked back out of the kitchen, she almost ran head-on into Sam. "Watch out! Sam! You aren't supposed to be back here!"

"I need to get out of here," he said, quickly turning his head from side to side, looking for an escape route.

"Why?"

"My ex just walked in and I gotta get out of here. Move over, doll, I'm coming through." Sam squeezed around her, then ran out of the back door, quietly closing it behind him.

Deloris looked toward the door and saw a blonde-haired woman scanning the restaurant, searching for someone. She assumed she was Sam's ex-wife. The man with her was doing the same, looking around.

Deloris walked over to the couple. "May I seat you at a table?"

The woman looked beautiful with her big blue eyes and bright red lips, but her face was twisted in anger. Her makeup looked carefully applied and her cheeks were slightly blushed. On her short, curly blonde hair, she wore a pillbox hat with a feather sticking out of it. A silver fox capelet was draped over her black, mid-calf evening dress. She was obviously dressed for a night out on the town.

Ignoring Deloris's question, she instead said, "Did you see a guy in here about this tall with brown hair and wearing a brown suit?"

"Why are you looking for him?"

"Answer the question!" the man interrupted gruffly.

Maybe," Deloris answered, taken aback by his abruptness.

"Look, honey, I need to find him. He's my ex-husband, and he stole something from me that I need back." She turned to the man and started to cry. Then she said, "If I get my hands on him, I'm going to kill him." She raised her hands and made a motion of strangling someone.

"I'm sorry, but he isn't here," Deloris replied.

Connie walked up to them. "Alice, what are you doing here?"

"I'm looking for Sam. Tony here says he heard he was here about an hour ago."

"What did he do this time?"

"He stole my mother's diamond brooch, and I assume he hocked it. If I find him, I'm going to kill him!" she screamed.

Connie took a deep breath and tried to calm Alice down. "Well, as you can see, he's not here. Do you want to have a seat and we can get you some special coffee to calm your nerves?" She took the woman's arm and tried to lead her to a table.

Alice yanked it away. "No! I need to find Sam!"

"Okay then, if you aren't going to order anything, then I need for you and Tony to leave." Putting her hands on her hips, she continued, "I can't have you upsetting my customers and my waitresses."

She motioned to Sal, who was ready to escort them out. When the couple saw Sal come from behind the bar, they left fairly quickly, with the men exchanging threatening looks. That was one time Deloris was glad that Sal had a threatening demeanor.

"Sorry, you had to see that, Deloris. I promise you that things are normally pretty quiet around here."

"Who is she?" Deloris asked, unable to resist.

"She is one of Sam Sloan's ex-wives, and that's her brother, Antonio Messino. I don't know why Sam ever married her. She's been bad news for him from the start."

"One of?"

"Yes, Johnny Lazia is married to another of Sam's ex-wives, Isabel."

"Johnny Lazia?"

"Yes, he is a very important man in Kansas City," Connie replied.

Before Deloris could ask her another question, the front door opened again.

"Oh, here are some customers," Connie noted. "I'll get them seated if you will take their orders."

"Right behind you," Deloris said with a nod.

"So, Sam has more than one ex-wife," Deloris thought to herself. "That figures, the big flirt. And who is Johnny Lazia? I need to ask Austin if he knows him."

Chapter Nine
Jules Stanford

The next night, Sam was back at the same table with his newspaper and Deloris served him black coffee.

He motioned her over to his table. "Can you give me the directions?"

"Directions?"

"Yea, the directions to your heart," Sam said with a wink.

Deloris rolled her eyes. "Look, I told you. I have a boyfriend."

"Well, dollface, if you decide to dump that boyfriend of yours, remember, we could be having a good time at the Pla-Mor."

"I'm sure we could," she said as she walked away, laughing and shaking her head.

At that moment, another couple walked into the restaurant, dressed to the nines. He looked like a million dollars and she was along for the ride, dripping in diamonds with a mink stole draped over her shoulders. Every eye in the place was on them.

Sam watched them, too, as they took a seat, and then resumed hiding behind his paper.

When Deloris returned to the kitchen, she asked Franny, "Who's that?" pointing the couple out through the serving window.

Franny peeked out the window and said, "That's Jules Stanford, rumored to be a silent partner in the Sugarhouse

Syndicate, started by his Grandfather Saperi and his mother's brothers."

"What's the Sugarhouse Syndicate?" Deloris asked, intrigued.

"You don't know about them?" In a low voice, Franny continued, "They provide sugar, among other ingredients, needed for alcohol. With the sugar shortage, they have a corner on the market. It's said that they also operate a few hundred stills, or maybe more, in the Kansas City area."

"Oh, I see," Deloris said, eyeing the couple.

"Yeah, be careful serving him. If he doesn't like your service, it could cost you your job here. He supplies Sal with his special blend of coffee."

"I will. Thanks for the warning." Deloris returned to the dining room and refilled Sam's coffee, but he was still totally engrossed in watching Jules Stanford and his date.

She went to Jules' table and asked for their order.

"I'll have the lasagna and my date here will have spaghetti and meatballs with a salad and some of Sal's special coffee for both of us."

Whenever a couple ordered the special blend of coffee, she learned to tell Sal, who would look around and then walk into the kitchen. Deloris followed him this time, pretending to put together a salad. Just inside the door to the kitchen on the left was a full-length shelf the size of a door that they stored supplies, like napkins, coffee cups, and a tray of bread. Also on the shelf was a wooden box. She saw Sal turn the wooden box and the shelf swung open like a door! Deloris's jaw dropped, and she stood there for a moment before walking over to look inside, but Sam then closed the door behind him. "This secret room must be where he stores and brews his secret coffee," she surmised. Deloris dumped the lettuce back in the bin and moved to one of the preparation tables to try and get a better look inside the room when he opened the door. She grabbed some silverware and acted like she was going back out to the customers, but she remained watching. Lucky for her, Franny and Olivia had their backs to her and didn't see her antics. Enzo was outside, putting the garbage in a metal can.

When Sal came back out to the kitchen, he carried a coffee pot. He set it down to grab two coffee cups and then poured the coffee into them. Noticing Deloris watching, he looked up at her and smiled. She had never seen him smile before, and it startled her. He said, "It's a special blend of coffee." Then he walked out to serve Jules and his girlfriend.

When their food was ready, Deloris brought it to them and asked, "Can I get you anything else?"

"That's all for now." Jules spoke with an air of authority. As Deloris walked away, he leaned over to say something in a low voice to the woman with him. Glancing back, Deloris saw her nod in agreement and then scan the patrons in the restaurant. From the back table, Sam caught the woman's eye, and she smiled at him sweetly before continuing to look around.

As she went into the kitchen, Deloris realized there was something slightly familiar about the woman, but Deloris couldn't put her finger on it. Maybe she'd seen her on the bus or at Poppy's, but she was sure she had seen her before. She peeked out of the serving window to watch the couple. Was she flirting with Sam? "That can't be with her boyfriend right there," she thought.

A short time later, Sam quietly slipped out of the restaurant through the kitchen door again.

At eight o'clock, the band—which consisted of two violins, a mandolin, a viola, and a cello—started playing soft music. They only played on Friday and Saturday nights. Another couple walked in, and then another. Soon, the restaurant was full of customers, resulting in Lilly and Deloris running around getting them all served. Thankfully, Deloris didn't have another incident of pinching that night, or if she did, she was too busy to notice.

After some dessert, Jules and his girlfriend danced and laughed and drank Sal's special coffee. As they were leaving, Jules gave Deloris a fifty-cent tip and told her good job. Relieved that he didn't have any problems with her service, she showed Lilly the tip.

"He is a good tipper," Lilly winked. The rest of the night went quickly, and before Deloris knew it, Connie was locking the doors. Deloris and Lilly cleaned the tables off and took the dirty dishes to the kitchen, where Enzo and Olivia were washing them. Sal put the chairs on top of the tables and Deloris and Lilly swept the floor, while Connie went to her office to count the proceeds.

Deloris went home tired that night, but satisfied that she did her best to keep up with Lilly and she felt that she did a pretty good job of it. After all, she did get a big tip, too.

Chapter Ten
Olive Oil

Sunday afternoon, Austin stopped by the boarding house. He found Deloris in the kitchen, fixing herself a bite to eat.

"Hey Austin, what brings you by? Do you want something to eat?"

"Naw, I just stopped to see how your new job went the last two nights," he said, leaning up against the kitchen counter.

"Why? Did you find something out about the Venetian Gardens or the Binaggios?"

"I didn't find much out. There are three brothers who immigrated from Sicily about 1905."

"I know Nino and Sal are brothers, but there's a third one?" Having finished putting together her sandwich for lunch, Deloris carried it to the dining room, motioning for Austin to follow.

"There was a third one, but he was mysteriously gunned down in the street a year ago," Austin explained, taking a seat at the table. "No one has been arrested for the crime and it remains unsolved. Nino had a few run-ins with the law, but only minor things like petty larceny. Other than that, Nino is pretty clean. Sal has a thicker record. He was arrested for suspected bootlegging and had several run-ins with the law. He was also suspected of murdering the third brother, but we couldn't make anything stick—not enough to hold him, anyway. So, watch yourself around them. Anyone who could kill his own brother, well, you know."

Deloris swallowed hard. "Wow, his own brother? I'll be careful, but I need this job, remember?"

"I know, just be careful. You never know what may happen next. Just last week we had to break up a fight that apparently involved a guy scamming another. The victim didn't take too well at losing and accused the grifter of cheating him out of his money with a fake bookie and a rigged horse race. The thing is, we found out later, that the victim thought he was in on the ground floor of the rigged horse race and was going to collect thousands. He got scammed by what we call the Kansas City Shuffle."

"By the way, do you know a fellow named Johnny Lazia?" Deloris asked.

"The Johnny Lazia? Yes. It's rumored he is the head of the Mafia in Kansas City, more powerful than Pendergast. Why? Was he in the restaurant? Did you serve him?"

"Oh no. Connie mentioned his name, like I should know him or of him."

"I repeat, be careful," Austin admonished.

That afternoon, Deloris arrived at the Venetian Gardens early again and got ready for the crowd of diners to arrive. A knock came to the back door and Deloris found herself the only person near it to answer.

"'Bout time someone answered the door." A young man burst through the door with two wooden boxes of bottles in his arms.

"I'm sorry," Deloris said. "I just walked into the kitchen. May I help you?"

"Yeah, uh, I got an order for Sal of, uh, olive oil."

"Sal isn't here, but we don't need any olive oil," Deloris said confidently.

"Are you sure about that?" he asked, shifting under the weight of the boxes.

"I'm sure," she replied.

The fellow then turned and walked away, glancing back over his shoulder.

He returned an hour later with the same wooden boxes and when Deloris answered the door again, he asked to see Sal. She was curious why the olive oil was for Sal, specifically.

At that moment, Connie came into the kitchen and said, "Sorry, I was a little late getting here. Just put the olive oil over there and I'll have Sal put it away. Here," she said, handing him a couple of hundred-dollar bills. "I'm a little short, but I'll have it after tonight's receipts."

"Hum, I'll need to tell the boss about it and the order you missed accepting earlier, that this gal said you didn't need," he said, pointing to Deloris.

Connie raised her eyebrows and looked at Deloris. Recovering quickly, she said, "I know, but I promise I'll have the rest of the money, and I'm sorry about missing you earlier. She's new. Just come back later."

Satisfied with her answer, he looked Deloris up and down appreciatively, smiled and walked out the door.

"Connie, you don't really need any olive oil, see?" Deloris

pointed to the bottles of olive oil in the pantry. "I'm sorry if I got you into trouble."

"I know, dear, but we can't turn down their delivery. It is our insurance policy that we won't run out."

Puzzled, Deloris closed the pantry door, shaking her head, and walked out into the dining area. Connie unlocked the front doors, and the customers started flooding in. Sam came sauntering in about six o'clock and sat at the same table in the back.

"Hi dollface, how's your boyfriend?"

"Still my boyfriend," Deloris replied.

"That's a shame. Hey, I'll take a menu this time and a cup of coffee."

"Here you go," Deloris said as she handed him a menu. She grabbed a coffee cup and the pot of coffee, then took both to his table.

As she poured the coffee, she said, "What can I get for you?"

"How about some of your time?" he said with a grin.

"Sam," she said, exasperated.

"Okay, okay," he put up his hands. "How about some veal spiedini with spaghetti on the side?"

When Deloris brought Sam his order, she saw that he was weaving a coin between his fingers while lost in thought. The coin looked unusual. As she put the plate down in front of him, she asked, "What do you have there?"

"Oh this?" He stopped and held the coin up. "I won this in a dice game."

"Aren't dice games illegal?"

"Yeah, well, this was just a little game among friends."

"May I see it?"

"Sure," Sam responded as he handed the coin over to Deloris, slightly pausing when he touched her hand.

She examined it closely and said, "This looks old. Is it valuable?"

"Nah. I was a chump to accept it as collateral on a bet, but I felt sorry for the old geezer."

"But not too sorry to take his money and this coin? Wasn't he upset about losing it?" she asked as she handed it back to him.

"Look Toots, I gotta eat too," he said with a wink. "He told me some cockamamie story about it being a family heirloom, belonged to his gramps or something like that from the old country. He had a snoot full, and it was hard to understand him with his accent, slurring his words and all."

"Then why didn't you give it back to him, if it belonged to his gramps? You said he was your friend, didn't you?"

"He came with a friend of mine. I didn't know him. Besides, I like the feel of the coin. It is just the right size and weight for me to do this." And he commenced rolling it through his fingers again.

Deloris walked back to the kitchen, shaking her head. Still, the coin intrigued her. It looked old, and the picture of the man on the front looked similar to one she saw in a history book when she was in high school. She decided to look it up at the library one day soon when she got off work at the switchboard.

That night, Deloris was determined to find out what was in Sal's special blend of coffee. When he came back with the coffee pot and left it in the kitchen, she picked it up and held it to her nose. She noticed an unfamiliar smell that was more like Old Man Jones' moonshine!

She noticed the shelf door didn't quite latch the last time Sal was in there, so she peeked inside the long, narrow room. On the wall to the right was another door that must have gone into the beverage and pool building next door. On the left were several shelves filled with bottles that looked like the olive oil bottles that the guy had delivered. "So, they are selling illegal liquor during Prohibition," Deloris muttered to herself, realizing that the "olive oil" delivery was how Sal got his liquor. There were at least five coffee pots on a shelf, too.

Franny caught her looking inside and said, "You better close that door before Connie or Sal catch you looking inside."

Deloris jumped back, saying, "Yes, ma'am."

She closed the shelf door quickly and hurried out of the kitchen to return taking the customers' orders.

Chapter Eleven

G-Men Raid

A week later, Sunday's crowd came after church and was mostly families, which meant they were more demanding for Deloris's attention than the Friday and Saturday night customers. Lilly came in with a new look: short and curly, bleach-blonde hair.

"You cut and colored your hair?" Deloris asked.

Laughing, Lilly replied, "Yeah, I decided that I needed a change. Besides, I hear men prefer blondes." She winked at Deloris and walked off to take an order.

At the end of the evening, she and Lilly were bussing the empty tables. A few customers were still in the restaurant, waiting for their food. Sal had gone into the room behind the shelf in the kitchen and Connie was in her office counting the receipts. Everything was quiet until five men in trench coats and hats with guns drawn came bursting in through the front door.

"Ladies and gentlemen, I am Special Agent Jerome Boyle and we are Federal Prohibition Agents. This is a raid," said the first man inside, who appeared to be in charge. Deloris had her back to the door when they entered and they startled her so badly that she nearly jumped out of her shoes. She whirled around to face them with her heart pounding so fast, she thought it would jump out of her chest. Agent Boyle, with his dark hair, pencil mustache and Fedora hat that he wore low over his wire-rimmed glasses, looked menacingly around the room.

"I need everyone to stay where you are. Everyone standing, find a table and sit, then I need everyone to put your hands on the table in front of you where I can see them." Turning to two of the men he came in the door with, he said, "You guys watch them." Then he walked into the kitchen, where Deloris heard Olivia scream. She heard Franny complaining loudly, "I've got food to cook. I can't stop or it will be ruined!"

"There'll be no more food served today, ma'am," came the reply.

Deloris figured these were some of the government men, G-men, she had read about in the newspapers. She remembered one in charge in Chicago was named Eliot Ness, who became famous when he arrested Al Capone. Deloris was scared to death. If it wasn't gangsters she had to watch for, it was G-men. What was a small-town girl doing in a joint like this?

Agent Boyle then came back out into the restaurant with Connie, Franny, Olivia, and Enzo in tow, all accompanied by another agent who must have come in through the back door. He directed them to have a seat at two empty tables and spread their hands on the table. Franny, Olivia, and Enzo all sat at one table. Olivia was crying and Franny was trying to comfort her, while Enzo sat stoically, watching the agents. Connie sat at a front table by herself.

Agent Boyle asked, "Is this everyone?"

Connie nodded yes, but sitting behind her, Enzo was looking at the kitchen, and they all heard a bottle fall. Deloris knew that an "olive oil" bottle must have fallen from a shelf inside the little room, but the agents looked puzzled.

"Well, well, well. There is someone else here." Looking

pointedly at two of his men, the lead agent said, "Do a complete search in the kitchen and come back to me with the results."

After a few moments, the agents returned, shrugging their shoulders and saying that they couldn't find anything. Agent Boyle went over to the wall behind the bar and started knocking on it. The hollow sound gave it away that the wall wasn't solid and something was behind it. He followed the hollow sound to the kitchen door.

He yelled, "Come out, or we'll tear this wall down!"

A commotion occurred in the kitchen and Deloris heard the back door slam shut. Sal must have made a run for it. Agent Boyle commanded two of his officers to go after the runner.

When the two agents returned ten minutes later, Sal was in their custody. He had his hands up with sweat running down his face and a look of exasperation. One of the agents pushed Sal with the muzzle of his gun and said, "Go over there and join the others."

Sal sat at the table with Connie in front of everyone else.

"Okay, NOW do we have everyone?"

"Yes, officer," Connie replied with an annoyed edge in her voice.

"As I said before, I am Special Agent Jerome Boyle with the Federal Income Tax and Prohibition Bureau, and these are my men," the lead agent explained. "Some people call us G-men. We heard you are selling illegal alcohol on the premises, and we are going to do a little search for it now." Looking at his suspects, he demanded, "Who's in charge here?"

"I am," Connie quickly replied.

"Are you going to show us what's behind this wall, or do we need to tear it down?"

Connie sighed, "Hold on. I'll take you inside."

Special Agent Boyle instructed two of his men to go with Connie while he and the other agents kept an eye on the group assembled at the tables.

After a few minutes, one agent returned with a bottle of olive oil and handed it to Boyle. He popped the lid off and took a sniff.

"Just as I suspected," he said, replacing the lid. "Okay, ladies and gentlemen, we are going to take a little trip down to the federal courthouse and jail."

"But Officer, I need to clean up the kitchen!" Franny protested.

"You can come back after we book you."

"Book us?!" Deloris exclaimed.

"Yes," he replied, looking at her suspiciously.

"I just started working here a little over a week ago and I haven't served alcohol to anyone," she protested. "I'm almost nineteen and my mother will kill me if I get arrested!"

"And I'm supposed to care about that?"

"I hoped you would take pity on me." Deloris tried to look as innocent as she could, fluttering her eyelashes at him, and he seemed to soften a little.

Then Lilly popped up beside her and said, "I'm innocent too, Officer. Can I go?"

"No!" And that ended any chance Deloris had to avoid being

arrested.

Everyone was loaded up in a paddy wagon that was waiting outside and taken downtown.

At the courthouse, the booking officer said, "Hey, sweetheart! What's your name? Dollface, I'm talking to you!"

Deloris was stunned and felt like she was awakening from a nightmare as she looked up into the booking officer's smiling face. She had to think quickly of a false name, so her sister or her mother wouldn't know about her arrest. Just last night, she had read an article in *Liberty Magazine* about the Spanish Armada with a person named O'Meara in it. That sounded good.

"My name is, uh, Doris Mmmm. O'Meara. Yes, O'Meara."

She was pretty proud of herself for coming up with that name on the spot. The meaning in Latin was "of the sea" and she hoped to see the sea one day.

"How do you spell that?"

"O apostrophe, capital M e a r a."

"All right, Miss O'Meara. Come over here and we'll get your fingerprints."

When they finished processing Deloris at the courthouse, it was too late to take a bus home, especially on a Sunday night. Not wanting to tell Thelma about this, she called who else— Austin. She walked down a block and asked him to pick her up there.

When he arrived, he said, "Deloris! What are you doing here?"

"They raided the restaurant, and I got swept up with

everyone else. Please don't tell Thelma or my mother," she pleaded.

"I don't know," he said, rubbing his chin in contemplation. "What's in it for me?"

"Come on, Austin. I'll owe you one, okay?"

"Only one?" he scoffed. "I think this is worth at least five."

"Two, and that's my final offer. Besides," she lowered her voice and looked around furtively, "I can keep an eye on this restaurant for you and the police. That's worth two right there."

"You know I don't like you working there. You could get hurt, and an example is this right here," Austin said, pointing repeatedly at the ground between them.

"Come on. Wouldn't it help to have someone on the inside?"

Austin relented, "Maybe. Let me talk to Jim and see what he says, but it will only be worth one if we do go with it."

"Okay. Some birthday this has been," Deloris lamented.

"It's not your birthday."

"It will be tomorrow and that is close enough," Deloris retorted.

At home, she found Annie and Gracie still awake and in the living room.

"You're getting home a little late, aren't you?" Annie asked.

"Yeah, I had a rough night. I'm going to bed." Her tone of voice did not invite further questions.

Deloris slowly climbed the stairs, with Annie and Gracie following her up.

Chapter Twelve
Birthday

When Deloris got home from the switchboard Monday afternoon, she discovered that Thelma was in the process of icing a cake that she baked for Deloris's birthday.

"Oh Thelma, you didn't need to get up from your nap early to bake me a cake!"

"It isn't every day my baby sister turns nineteen," Thelma said with a smile. "I wanted it to be a surprise, but knew you'd be home before I finished. I took the day off at the diner so I could make your favorite foods: meatloaf, mashed potatoes, and green beans."

"It is such a lovely gesture, thank you. I am very thankful to spend my birthday with you." She reached out to hug her older sister.

"Oh, I invited Austin to join us for tonight's dinner," Thelma added.

"Wonderful!"

Later that evening, everyone had a pleasant time visiting and asking how Deloris's new job was going at the Venetian Gardens. Austin winked at her, and she told them about Connie and Sal, Lilly, Franny, Olivia, and Enzo. She left out the raid and the olive oil deliveries.

Annie spoke up, "Venetian Gardens? Didn't I hear about a raid at that place last night? G-men made some arrests. Were you there?"

"Oh uh, yeah they uh, they raided the place," Deloris stammered, avoiding Thelma's gaze. She glanced over to see that Thelma's face was as red as her hair, and Leota was sitting at the end of the table trying to hide a smile with her napkin.

"Deloris! Why didn't you tell me?" Thelma demanded.

Deloris's face turned red, too. "Because I knew you'd be upset."

Annie interrupted, "So you were arrested?!"

"Well, uh, I was fingerprinted and booked, but they let me go. I told them that I had just started working there."

"We can't let our mother know," Thelma almost cried.

"Oh, she probably won't know. I gave them a false name. I am Doris O'Meara. So, it will be okay. Don't be upset."

Deloris was saved from further interrogation by a knock at the door. She jumped up to answer it and discovered Leon standing there with a bouquet of flowers.

"This is very sweet of you. We are just about to have cake and ice cream. Can you stay?" she asked, eager for a way to deflect Thelma's ire.

"Sorry, doll, but I need to shuffle off to Chicago and I leave by train tonight. I just wanted to bring these by to you first." He handed her the bouquet of red roses.

"They're lovely," Deloris said, smelling them. "Thank you. Have a safe trip."

After watching Leon walk back to his car, Deloris returned to the dining room and put the flowers in the middle of the table. Everyone commented on how lovely they were, which broke a little of the uneasiness, but Thelma still had a scowl on her face looking at Deloris. Then came another knock on the door. Deloris went to answer it and found Les standing there wearing a Western Union hat and smiling mischievously. Thank goodness he didn't come earlier and run into Leon.

"Western Union telegram for Miss Deloris Markham. Are you the recipient?"

Laughing, Deloris replied, "Yes, it is I. I am Deloris Markham."

He handed her the telegram, and she opened it. Included inside were two tickets to the movies. He said, "Dinner and a movie tomorrow night?"

"Please reply that I'd be honored to go out to eat and go to a movie with Les Wells. Stop." She and Les both laughed. Then she said, "Would you like to stay for some cake and ice cream?"

"Why, yes. I'd like that."

Having Les there cut some of the tension of the evening. Before leaving, he pulled Deloris into the kitchen to tell her goodbye and give her a hug and a kiss. "I'll see you later, DeDe."

"Yes, I'll see you later," she swooned.

Ten minutes later, when Austin left, he wished Deloris a happy birthday and added, "I guess we need to keep an eye out for this Doris O'Meara. She sounds like a dangerous character."

"You do that," Deloris responded as she hit him on his shoulder, pushing him out of the door.

In the kitchen, Gracie, Leota, and Annie did the clean-up and washed the dishes while Thelma and Deloris went into the living room.

"We need to talk," Thelma began. "I can't have you keeping secrets from me. As sisters we should be able to tell each other anything."

"I was going to tell you, but I hadn't found the right time," Deloris pleaded. "I promise I will tell you everything from now on in the future."

They hugged and Thelma got ready to go to work.

Chapter Thirteen

The Special Blend Coffee

The next weekend at Venetian Gardens brought pretty much the same crowds, and Sam showed up at least twice on Friday and Saturday. Connie and Sal had a talk with everyone to tell them that Sal's special blend of coffee would not be served for a while, only regular coffee.

Midway through the evening on Friday, a gentleman dressed in expensive clothes walked in with a blonde on his arm. They were flanked by two men, who were obviously packing guns. Sal came from behind the bar to greet them and seated them himself. He snapped his fingers to Deloris to come and take their order.

"What can I get you to drink?" she asked the man.

"We'll have two of Sal's special blends of coffee." Deloris swallowed hard. "I'm sorry, sir, but we are out of that coffee."

"What? No special blend? That's not good."

"I'm sorry, sir. Can I get you two regular coffees?"

"Well, I guess if you can't get me two of the special blends of coffee, we'll just go somewhere else that does serve us that." They rose from the table and he put the woman's mink coat over her shoulders. The other two men stood up from a nearby table where they were seated and the whole entourage exited.

Sal hurried over. "What happened?"

"They wanted your special blend of coffee, and I had to tell them we were out."

"What? For them, I could still supply some from a hidden bottle I have under the bar. Why didn't you come and tell me?"

Deloris blinked. "I, I thought we were out. I didn't know you had a hidden bottle. Who was he anyway?"

Sal didn't answer her, instead yelling "Johnny!" and running outside, but it was too late to catch them.

Sam was sitting at his usual table in the back, witnessing all of this, when Nino came into the restaurant and strode directly back to him.

"What did you do?" Nino demanded. "Did you tell Johnny Lazia to come in tonight?"

"I didn't do anything," Sam retorted.

"I know you told the Feds!" Nino said as he pushed a chair hard into the table where Sam was seated.

"No, no, I didn't!"

More angry words were spoken, and an argument escalated until Nino grabbed Sam by the arm and stood him up.

"I don't want you in here anymore, anyway. I don't want your old lady or any of your ex-wives and their goombahs coming in here and causing trouble, harassing my staff," Nino said angrily, wagging a finger in Sam's face. "You need to leave or I'll have Sal throw you out the door."

"I'm going," Sam said angrily as he straightened his suit coat and tie. At the door, he turned and threatened, "You're going to regret this."

Deloris didn't know why Nino thought Sam told the G-men about the illegal hooch, but Sam didn't come back. However, his ex-wife, Alice, and her brother showed up again an hour later. This time, Nino stopped them at the door.

"He's not here, so you need to turn around and leave before Sal escorts you out again."

Angrily, the siblings turned and walked out of the door.

The fellow with the special order of olive oil didn't come at his usual time, and she saw Sal stash a couple of guns behind the bar. If a dish was dropped, Connie would jump. If the door was slammed shut from a powerful gust of wind, Sal would start to reach for the guns behind the bar. Connie and Nino huddled at the table in the back corner of the restaurant, talking in whispers. Everything seemed very tense at the Venetian Gardens, and everyone appeared to be nervous.

Chapter Fourteen

The Mafia Calling Card

The date of September 26, 1931, was one Deloris would remember for years to come. She went to work as usual that Saturday night. Two customers came in right at closing and ordered some food for takeout. They sat at a table closest to the bar. As the restaurant was closing for the evening, Nino came by to pick up Connie. He had just walked in the door when suddenly, Sal yelled out, "Get down!" Bullets started flying into the restaurant from the street.

Deloris whipped around to look out the serving window and saw Sal pulled the guns and a hammer from behind the bar and run to the window at the end of the bar. He broke the glass out, then started shooting out of the window back at the assailants.

Franny pulled Deloris down behind the sink. Crouched in the kitchen, Olivia and Enzo were hiding behind the door to the freezer and Olivia was hysterical, yelling something in Italian. Lilly ran into the kitchen and duck behind the refrigerator. Another barrage of bullets rang out and when it everything was quiet, they came out of the kitchen to see the restaurant in shambles. Nino was shot in the chest and Connie was hovering over him, trying to stop the bleeding. Sal ran outside and started firing both guns back at a car that was speeding away. Franny, Lilly, and Deloris rushed out of the kitchen to assess the damage and to see how Nino and Connie were doing. Deloris was horrified to see that Connie had blood on the front of her blouse from Nino, but also blood on her shoulder.

"You're hurt!" Deloris yelled out.

"No, I'm fine, but we need to get an ambulance for Nino. He's hurt bad." She turned back to him, cradling his head in her lap. "Nino baby, hang on. We're going to get help."

Nino looked up into Connie's eyes and said weakly, "I thought I fixed it. I'm sorry, baby."

Connie gave him a kiss and said, "It's okay, Nino. It's okay. Just hang on."

Nino slumped in Connie's arms. Deloris felt for a pulse on Nino's neck and discovered there was none. She slowly shook her head at Connie, who then burst into tears. Sal came back into the restaurant saying something in Italian and hobbling with one leg bleeding.

"We need to call the police," Deloris said in anguish and started to stand up to run to the phone in Connie's office.

"No police!" Connie yelled, grabbing Deloris's hand and pulling her down next to her on the floor.

"But..." Deloris protested.

"No police!" Connie repeated, halfway standing and more strongly this time, looking at Deloris straight in the eye.

"We still need to get you to a hospital to get you looked at and look at Sal's leg over there! He should have it looked at as well. Plus, we need the ambulance to come pickup Nino..." her voice softened. "And you know the police will come with it."

Sobbing, Connie shrunk down next to Nino's body and nodded her head in agreement. Despite Connie's request, the police showed up, along with the ambulance, after Deloris called.

"Who's in charge here?" a powerful voice came from the doorway.

Deloris looked up into a familiar face. There stood Big Jim with notebook in hand, and Austin behind him. Deloris was never so glad to see those two in her life. Big Jim hadn't seen Deloris yet in the dimly lit restaurant, consequently she stood up and replied, "She is," while pointing to Connie, still slumped on the floor. "But as you can see, she is in no shape to answer questions just yet."

"Deloris!" Big Jim exclaimed, startled, as his eyes adjusted to the dim light. "What are you doing here?"

Austin looked at Deloris and stepped up. "Are you okay?" He put a hand on her shoulder.

"Yes, I'm fine. Just shook up, that's all," she answered with a shudder.

"Okay then." Before walking away, he mouthed, "I told you so," and started questioning Olivia and Enzo, who were sitting at a table in the back corner. Enzo was in shock, and Olivia was crying hysterically. Austin managed to get her calmed down before he began his questions.

Deloris could hear Olivia respond in broken English to his questions with a raised voice, "I don't see nothin' but bullets. I don't get involved in nothin'. I just cook. Okay?"

"I repeat, what are you doing here?" Big Jim asked Deloris with a slight irritation in his voice as she turned her attention back to him.

"I work here," she said as she looked around the restaurant. "Or I worked here."

"Since when?"

"I started here right after Poppy's closed down for the season."

From the floor where she still sat next to her husband's body, Connie, who had stopped crying, interrupted, "You know these guys?!"

"Oh, uh yes, I grew up with that officer over there," Deloris said as she pointed at Austin, still not wanting to tell Connie that she also worked at the KCPD switchboard.

Big Jim turned to Connie. "Ma'am, are you hurt?" he asked, concerned.

Deloris answered for her, "Yes, she was shot in her shoulder when the shooting started and Sal, over there, ran after them. I guess they shot him in the leg because he came back in here hobbling and bleeding after they sped off."

"Thank you, Deloris," Big Jim replied, slightly agitated that she didn't give Connie a chance to talk. "Let me help you up," he said to Connie as he took her by her uninjured arm and guided her to a chair. He motioned for an ambulance attendant to come and start administering to her wounds. "I am very sorry for your loss."

Connie started crying again, and Big Jim offered her a handkerchief. "Thank you. He protected me, you know. He stood in front of me and took all the bullets."

"Do you mind if I ask you a few questions while they work on bandaging your shoulder?" Jim asked softly. She shook her head no. "Thank you. What is your name?"

"Connie," she replied in a raspy voice.

"Okay, Connie. Did you get a look at the shooters?"

"No," she whispered. "It all happened so fast, and Nino blocked my view."

"I understand. So, you don't know how many of them there were or the car or anything like that?"

"No."

"All right. What is your last name?"

"Binaggio, Constance Binaggio."

"Would you spell that, please?"

"B I N A G G I O."

"Thank you, ma'am. If you think of anything, here is my name and again, I am very sorry." He handed Connie a piece of paper with his name written on it.

Meanwhile, Austin went over to the two customers who had been waiting for a to go order when the shooting started and started questioning them. They told him they ducked behind the bar when the shooting started and didn't really see anything. Austin took their information and told them that they could leave. Then he walked over to Lilly, who had been sitting on the floor a few feet away from Connie.

He offered her a hand and when she stood up, her legs collapsed under her, or so it appeared, throwing her into Austin's arms. With her arms around his neck and looking into his eyes, she said, "I guess I'm a little woozy. I think I need to sit down, too."

He blushed and guided her to a chair. "Why don't you sit here a minute and relax, ma'am, and I'll go ask that fellow over there some questions."

Grabbing his arm and stopping him, Lilly said, "Oh, I'll be

fine, and I'm not a ma'am, by the way. I'm a miss," she quickly added.

"Okay, can I get you a glass of water or anything, miss?"

"Your number would be nice."

"Uh, yes. Well, oh, here is a glass of water," he said as he took the glass from Olivia, who had heard the request. "Okay, miss. May I ask you a few questions?"

"Yes, you may, Sugar. I mean, sir," she said with a wicked gleam in her eye and then a wink.

Ignoring her, Austin asked, "What is your name?"

"Lillibeth Ross, but I go by Lilly," she said, watching him write her name down.

"What can you tell me about the shooting?"

"I was wiping the tables down and waiting for the last order. Nino had just walked in. He hadn't closed the door yet, and Connie went over to greet him. That's when the shooting started. I hit the floor, and that's where you found me a minute ago. I was afraid to get up. Sal, over there, ran out the door after them. When he came back in, he was bleeding." She took a drink of water after that string of words.

Her statement surprised Deloris because she knew Lilly ran into the kitchen and hid behind the refrigerator. She wasn't on the floor, but Deloris figured Lilly was in a state of shock and might not remember that exactly.

"Did you see the shooters?"

"I saw a guy riding on the running board and hanging on with one arm and a Tommy gun in the other."

"A Tommy gun, huh?" Austin asked, raising an eyebrow. "How did you know it was a Tommy gun?"

"Well, I read a lot, see? And I go to the movies, see? And I know gangsters prefer Tommy guns and women, see?" she said, mimicking Edward G. Robinson with a wink.

"Very funny."

"What? Haven't you seen *Smart Money* with James Cagney and Edward G. Robinson yet? Maybe you should take me and I'll tell you all about it, see?" She smiled coquettishly.

Austin blushed again. "Uh, yes, Miss Ross, could you describe the guy with the Tommy gun?" He focused on his notepad.

"Not really," she said with a shrug. "It all happened very fast, and he had his hat pulled low over his face." Lilly looked genuinely sorry that she couldn't tell him more.

"Okay, thank you." He closed his notepad. "We'll be in touch if we need anything else from you."

"I hope you do, Officer," she said, fluttering her eyelashes at Austin. She cupped her curly blonde hair like Mae West often did in the movies.

Deloris, standing nearby, heard this exchange and started shaking her head with silent laughter. She had never seen Austin look this flustered. He looked sternly at Deloris and mouthed for her to cut it out.

Franny stood up from the table nearby. "Hello, Officer? Can you please talk to me? I want to take my son and sister home? They are pretty shaken up." She put her hand on Enzo's shoulder.

Big Jim walked over to where Franny was standing. "Certainly. What's your name?"

"I'm Franny. Francesca Casciola. I've worked here since it opened. Nino and Connie Binaggio are my neighbors and I've known them for years. They didn't deserve this. They are good people, just trying to make a living."

"I understand. What can you tell me about the shooters?"

"I can't. I was in the kitchen cooking the last customers' meals and cleaning up when I heard the shots. I quickly ducked down behind the sink. It's steel, you know. Nothing gets through it." She continued, "I pulled Deloris down beside me because she was standing there trying to look out the window."

Shaking his head, Big Jim looked at Deloris, and in a reprimanding tone, said, "Deloris."

Defending herself, she said, "I've never been in a shooting before! I wanted to see who was shooting so that I could give you a thorough description." She put both palms of her hands up and shrugged her shoulders after saying that.

"You could have been shot with bullets flying all over the place!" Austin protested as he walked up. Deloris's parents had asked Austin to protect her in the city, and he found that to be much harder than he expected when he agreed to do it.

Deloris avoided his gaze. "I know that now," she said sheepishly.

"Did you get a description?" Austin asked her pointedly.

"Not really," she admitted. "Franny pulled me down before I got a good look. All I got was a quick glimpse of a guy hanging out of a car."

"Can you describe him?"

"No," she answered, looking miserable.

Shaking his head, Austin walked over to talk with Sal now that he was bandaged up. He sat on a barstool with one arm resting on the bar and his other hand rubbing his head, showing his disbelief at the recent events.

Deloris inched a little closer to hear their conversation.

"And what is your name?"

"You don't need my name. I need you to go after the *mascalzones* who did this and quit wasting our time!" Sal yelled out in frustration, slamming his fist on the bar.

"Do you know who did this?" Austin persisted.

"Yeah, but I can't tell you. The walls have ears."

"Then how are we going to stop them, if you don't tell me?"

"We have our own justice system."

"I don't want to hear that," Austin said, rolling his eyes. "You gotta give me something if you want real justice."

Sal finally looked at Austin. "Okay, talk with Sam Sloan."

"Why Sam?"

"He got into an argument with Nino and Nino threw him out with a warning to never come back. He turned and yelled at Nino that he'd be sorry. He has *goombahs*, you know, friends that could have done this. If you don't find him and I find him first..." Sal's voice trailed off and he slid a finger across his throat.

"Settle down there. What's your name again?"

"Sal. Nino was my brother."

"What is your full name?"

"You don't need that. Just find the *malfattore*, Sam Sloan."

"Okay," Austin relented. "Where will I find Sam?"

"I don't know. I hear he has a buddy who works at the Riverside Race Track. Check there."

Big Jim walked up to Austin and asked, "Did you get what you need?"

"I think so. Thank you, Mr. uh Binaggio, right?" Sal nodded his head that he had in both hands now. Closing his notebook, Austin turned to Connie and said, "Do you need a ride home?"

"No, thank you, Officer. Sal and I will get a ride with a friend that I can call. Franny can give Lilly, Olivia, and Enzo a ride."

"Okay, how about you, Deloris? Do you need a ride home?"

"That'd be great. But wait. Do you need me to help clean up some of this mess, Connie?"

"No. Tonight we're just going to close and lock the door, or what's left of it, if it will even lock," Connie answered sadly. "I think we all need to just go home."

"Okay, I'll be back tomorrow to help you clean up, then." Deloris went into the office to get her coat and purse, then time out. As she turned to leave, she glanced down and saw a crumpled piece of paper in the waste bin. She grabbed one of her gloves out of her purse and put it on before removing the paper. She quickly stashed it in her purse and turned to walk out just as Lilly walked in.

Chapter Fifteen

The Ride Home

S o, what's with you and the police?" Lilly asked Deloris as she took her purse and coat out of her locker.

"Austin and Big Jim? Well, Austin and I grew up more like brother and sister. Our mothers are best friends. I've gone to lunch with Austin a few times and met Big Jim there. He's taken me home a few times." Deloris decided she wasn't lying, just omitting details of her relationship with Austin and Big Jim at the police department.

"I see. So, you and Austin, you ain't a thing?"

"Oh no. Like I said before, he's more like my brother." They giggled as they exited the office.

"I'm ready to go," Deloris said to Big Jim as she walked toward the door.

Big Jim turned to the assembly of people and said, "You are all free to go. If any of you think of anything you feel is important to this case, here is my name and number. Please contact me or Officer Martin here." Big Jim handed Connie a piece of paper he tore from his notepad.

Lilly turned to Austin and Big Jim and said, "Any chance this girl could hitch a ride home with you, too?"

Big Jim looked slightly disappointed, because he was probably planning to question Deloris for more information on the situation at the restaurant, but that could wait. Austin had a half smile and half grimace on his face.

"Sure thing, Miss, uh..." Big Jim replied.

"Ross, Lilly Ross," she replied as they all left the restaurant.

"Okay, Miss Ross. Where to?" Big Jim asked as the group took seats in the squad car.

"814 Olive Street." At that, Lilly settled back in the seat. "I never rode in a police car before. I mean, we rode in the paddy wagons when the G-men raided, but not a police car. Have you ridden in a police car before?" she asked Deloris.

"Well, as I said before, the guys have taken me home a few times."

"Oh yes," Lilly replied with a smile as she gazed at the back of Austin's head with interest.

When they arrived at Lilly's apartment building, Austin jumped out and opened the door for her.

"All that handsome and a gentleman too," she said demurely as she held onto the hand that Austin offered to help her out of the car. Then she added with a wink, "Don't forget my address, handsome. I'm free tomorrow night—now."

"Yes, ma'am. I mean, miss," he quickly corrected himself as he averted his eyes from her.

She turned around when she reached her door and said, "Oh, and my number is Wabash 148. That's Wabash 148." Then she blew him a kiss and turned with a flip of her skirt before entering the building.

As he pulled the car away, Big Jim and Deloris burst into uproarious laughter.

"What?" Austin rebutted.

"You've got an admirer, and she wants you," Big Jim teased.

"Nah, she's just still in shock."

"Well, I know Lilly and she goes after what she wants and usually gets him," Deloris added with a grin.

"Okay, okay. How about we focus on what happened tonight?" Austin quickly changed the subject. "What can you tell us about the Binaggios and their restaurant? Anything there that is suspicious or may have spurred this attack?"

"Well, let's see. There is a shelf in the kitchen that is actually a door to a small room where I'm pretty sure Sal has a secret stash of alcohol in bottles labeled as olive oil hidden inside... or rather, he did have alcohol hidden inside."

She looked at Austin and then back at Big Jim and continued, "Austin may have told you that the place was raided last week by G-men and they confiscated all of the 'olive oil.' Sal claimed to have a few bottles hidden somewhere else for special customers. Anyway, when customers came in and ordered his special blend of coffee, he went to the kitchen, moved the wooden box, and the door opened to this little room. He went inside and came out with a coffeepot that he filled with the alcohol. Then he poured the 'special blend coffee' into coffee cups and served them. He never let me serve them the 'coffee.'"

"Have you seen where the alcohol comes from?" Big Jim asked.

"I can't be certain. He is very secretive about its origin, but there is something strange about the olive oil. One day, a guy came delivering bottles of it. At least olive oil is what he called them, but I think they were actually bottles of alcohol. I thought it was strange when the G-men raided—one of them came out of Sal's hiding spot carrying a bottle of olive oil and another came back carrying a case of it."

"Why did you think they were alcohol?" Big Jim's eyes met hers in the rearview mirror.

"Because we already had a full pantry of olive oil, so I turned them away. They came about a week later and I started to turn them away again, but Connie caught them before they left. She told them we would take the order. Then I noticed Sal took that olive oil to his secret hideaway, where he made the special blend of his coffee. Oh, and when Special Agent Boyle took a whiff of the contents, that was when he hauled us all off to the federal courthouse."

"Interesting."

"Don't you see? We didn't need olive oil at all, but she told me we had to take the delivery. It seemed that bad things would happen if we didn't take it." Deloris's voice grew louder. "What if I brought this attack on because I sent the fellow away the first time?"

"I highly doubt that you caused them to attack," Big Jim replied, shaking his head. "It usually takes more than that."

After a moment, Deloris added, "Oh, I almost forgot. I found a crumpled-up piece of paper in Connie's office that she had thrown away." She put her gloves back on. Thank goodness she had them in her purse, because the fall nights could be chilly. She pulled the paper out of her purse. Austin reached to grab it and she scolded, "Fingerprints!"

"All right, then what does it say?" Austin asked.

"I don't know. I haven't read it yet." She carefully unfolded the paper and read it: "YOU MISSED YOUR LUG TAX. CHE PECCATO - TOO BAD!"

"Oh dear. I might be responsible, since I told them we didn't need the olive oil." Deloris's brow furrowed. "I guess *Che Peccato* means too bad, but what is a Lug Tax?"

"It can't be over a delivery of olive oil. Relax, that won't be all there is with this attack. There must be more," Big Jim said.

Feeling a little better, she sat back in the seat.

"What about this, Sam?" Austin asked.

"Sam? I don't think he had anything to do with this. He seems harmless enough to me," Deloris shrugged.

"Sal seemed to think he was responsible. What can you tell us about him? A description?"

"Other than the average Joe, he is about your height and weight, Austin, with brown hair and blue eyes. He wears a brown suit, with a brown hat and shoes. He is always twiddling with a coin, weaving it between his fingers. He says he won it off a poor man who gambled it away. That reminds me, I need to look that coin up and see if it is valuable. I'll do that Monday."

"That's it?" Austin pressed.

"Well, he likes to flirt a lot. But I guess that won't help you find him."

"No. Here's your stop. Try to stay out of trouble, will you?" Big Jim admonished.

Deloris climbed out of the squad car. "Me, Officer? I can't help if trouble comes looking for me." She fluttered her eyelashes and touched her chin with one finger in a flirtatious way, then turned and dashed up the sidewalk to her door before they could say anything else.

The next day, true to her word, Deloris returned to the Venetian Gardens to help clean up the mess. She helped Sal and a friend of his put boards across the broken door and window.

"So how are you doing, Sal? How's your leg?"

"I'll be okay. Just a flesh wound," he said, seeming to halfway be friendly to her.

"The cane makes you look distinguished," Deloris said with a smile.

"Well, I don't feel distinguished," he said with a grimace.

"So, who do you think did this?"

"Like I told the officers last night, I think Sam Sloan is at the bottom of it with his goombahs, or it could be someone from the Sugarhouse Syndicate."

"The Sugarhouse Syndicate? That doesn't sound dangerous." She feigned ignorance to see what Sal would say.

"Why don't you go talk to the Saperi brothers or Lazia and see just how dangerous the Sugarhouse Syndicate truly is? I..."

Sal's friend interrupted, mumbling, "*Chiudere il becco, Omerta,*" and Sal shut up.

After everything was picked up, cleaned up, and put in some sort of order, Deloris went to Connie and asked, "Do you know how long before you can reopen the restaurant?"

"Oh, honey, I don't think that we will reopen the restaurant,"

Connie answered with a deep sigh. "The damage is one thing, but losing Nino was the final straw. I'm sorry. If you come back to the office, I'll give you your final paycheck."

"I understand. I'm very sorry for your losses. This was a devastating blow in so many ways."

With Big Jim and Austin investigating Sam, the Sugarhouse Syndicate, and Sal Binaggio, Deloris remembered she was going to look into the coin that Sam had. She decided to do that tomorrow. When she arrived home that evening, she went to Annie, who was obviously working on a story, and asked, "Hey do you want to go with me to the library tomorrow to look up a coin? This fellow that came into the Venetian Gardens owns it and it looks old. I'm just curious about it."

"Sure, what time?" Annie asked as she gathered all her papers and put them into a satchel.

They made the arrangements to meet after Deloris finished her shift at the switchboard.

Chapter Sixteen

The Coin

The next afternoon, Deloris took the bus to Ninth and Locust to meet Annie. Deloris remembered reading an article in the newspaper about the library and the head librarian, Mr. Purd Wright. It said that the two-story Italian Renaissance style building was built in 1895 when Kansas City outgrew the original building located at Eighth and Oak Streets. Deloris stepped back to admire the building with the limestone bottom and light-colored masonry top. Two Doric style columns graced the arched entrance with four more at the other two porticos on the side. Above the entrance was a balcony with six more Doric style columns. It was a beautiful building. She opened the heavy oak door at the entrance and found Annie waiting inside.

"Let's ask the librarian for some ideas about where to search for rare coins," Annie suggested.

An occasional creak emitted from the oak wood floors as they walked by the slanted shelves filled with books in the center area where the main desk and librarian were found, sitting within six marble columns and a marble fireplace on the wall behind.

The librarian recommended they head for the rare collections book section. After searching through several coin books, Deloris finally found the coin.

"Here it is!" she said triumphantly. "It is an *Eid Mar or Denarius of Brutus also known as The Ides of March coin.*"

Showing Annie the page, she pulled out a sketchbook and drew it. "How does this look?"

"Pretty good. What does it say about it?"

"Apparently, Brutus minted the coin to commemorate the slaying of Julius Cesar." Deloris read the information from the book:

> The **Ides of March coin**, also known as the **Denarius of Brutus** or **EID MAR**, is a rare version of the denarius coin issued by Marcus Junius Brutus from 43 to 42 BC. The coin was struck to celebrate the March 15, 44 BC, assassination of Julius Caesar. It features a bust of Brutus on one side and a pileus cap between two daggers on the other. The coin was minted in both silver and gold. Approximately 100 of the silver coins are known to exist, but only three of the gold examples have survived. The coin is considered one of the rarest ancient Roman coins.[1]

"Oh, my goodness. That's old. I bet it is worth a fortune!" Deloris exclaimed. "I can't imagine Sam just twirling it between his fingers. He may not know how valuable it is."

"Let's go to a rare coin collector and ask the owner about the coin and how much it is worth," Annie suggested, pulling another volume. "Here is the city directory. We can look one up in here."

Inside a rare collectibles shop, they looked around as they waited for the gentleman who worked there to finish with a customer.

When it came time, Annie told him she was a reporter with

The Kansas City Post and was doing some research for a story. Deloris then showed him her sketch and described the coin to him. From his raised eyebrows, they could tell that he was intrigued.

"Do you have it with you? I can give you a more accurate estimate, if I see it?" he asked eagerly. "It could be a reproduction. There are several, you know, and I find it hard to believe this rare coin made it to Kansas City, Missouri."

"No, I only have this drawing that I made from a book at the library. How can we look for a fake?"

"Look for the pileus cap between two daggers on one side, and the bust of Brutus with the correct markings of BRVT IMP and L PLAET CEST on the other side. If it has that and is silver, then the coin is valuable. If it is gold, it is even more rare and valuable."

"And what is a pileus cap?" Annie asked.

"It is a felt cap with no brim that was typically worn by Ancient Greeks and Egyptians. Kind of like the hat the Shriners wear."

"I see."

"And you say that the coin is valuable?" Deloris asked.

"Yes. The gold one is the most valuable coin in the world."

"Really?" the girls looked at each other in surprise.

"If you get possession of it, I'd like to see it."

"Yes, thank you for the information," Deloris said as she walked to the door and the two of them exited the shop. They started talking in excited tones about the information.

"Hey, Deloris, I'd love to stick around, but I need to go back to the paper to work on a story. This has been exciting. I'll see you at home later."

"Don't say or write anything about the coin, okay?"

"Oh, I won't."

"Okay, I'll see you then."

Annie headed toward the newspaper office, leaving Deloris at the bus stop alone.

Chapter Seventeen

What Are Friends For?

As Deloris rode the bus home, she said to herself, "Well, guess I am looking for a job again. I'd better get started. I'll grab the Sunday paper from yesterday and start going through the Want Ads."

That evening, she started perusing the want ads. There were bookkeepers and typists wanted, but Deloris hadn't taken either class at Jameson. Cosmetic demonstrator might be a possibility. Nope, that is a Monday through Friday job in the mornings and that would conflict with her switchboard job, plus she would need to apply makeup to actors and actresses. She had zero experience doing that, even though she was in two plays in high school. She faked her way into working at a soda fountain, but this required a certain expertise that she didn't have, because she never wore makeup except lipstick.

One looked intriguing: "Wanted: Demonstrators capable of calling on women's clubs, parent-teachers, etc. for the latest scientific hygienic corporation." She wondered what that might be about, so she circled it. Maid and housekeeping work didn't exactly appeal to her. She wanted something more interactive with other people. She enjoyed working with the public. She found a saleslady position where they will train. "Here's another one that looked promising," she thought, "Waitress wanted at a local diner." She circled that one.

When Deloris got home from the switchboard the next afternoon, she grabbed the Sunday newspaper and went to the phone to call. She had marked the jobs in order of interest and began calling the numbers. When she told them she was looking for weekends or afternoons only, they either told her they needed someone weekdays in the morning, they didn't have weekend hours, or she needed experience. She was down to the last one.

"Hello, I am calling about the waitress position you advertised in the newspaper. Already filled? Oh, I see. Thank you anyway." Disappointed, Deloris returned to the couch and sat back, releasing a sigh of resignation.

Unexpectedly, there came a knock at the door. Deloris answered it and was surprised to see Stella and Trudie.

"Why so glum?" Trudie asked.

"Oh, I've been calling around trying to get an interview for a job with no luck."

"Why don't you call my Nona and ask her?" Stella questioned. "Remember, I told you about it. The Indiana Gardens on Indiana Avenue."

Deloris smacked her palm to her forehead. "I totally forgot about you telling me that. What is the telephone number? I will call there tomorrow."

Once she gave her the number, Stella said, Her name is Sicilia Martinelli, not Cecilia. It is S I C I L I A. She is named after Sicily, where she was born.

"Got it. I believe I can remember that."

"Hey, let's all go to the movies, unless you have a date tonight, Deloris."

"No, I don't." Deloris stuck her tongue out at Stella and

continued. "Sounds good to me. What are we going to see?"

"I want to see *Three Who Loved* starring Conrad Nagel at the Uptown Theater. He is very handsome," Trudie swooned. "I saw him in *One Romantic Night* and fell in love."

"You fall for all the leading men," Stella teased, and Trudie's cheeks turned a bright pink as she looked down in embarrassment.

Breaking the momentary silence, Deloris said, "All right. Just let me get changed and I'll be out in a jiffy."

A few minutes later, grabbing her hat and purse, Deloris said, "Okay, I'm ready to go."

Chapter Eighteen
Indiana Gardens Restaurant

“T”he next afternoon, Deloris dug into her purse and produced the piece of paper Stella had written the Indiana Gardens phone number on. She waited until it was two o'clock to call the restaurant, hoping that their noonday rush would slow or be over.

“Hello, may I speak with Mrs. Sicilia Martinelli?”

“Nona! *Telephono!*”

“Allo?”

Nervously, Deloris blurted out, “Hello, Mrs. Martinelli. My name is Deloris Markham and my friend, your granddaughter, Stella, told me that I might get a job as a waitress there.” She then waited for her response.

Mrs. Martinelli responded, “*Non capisco.*” Then the line went dead, after Mrs. Martinelli apparently hung up.

Deloris waited a few minutes and then called back. The same youthful voice answered the phone.

“Hello, my name is Deloris Markham and my friend, Stella Martinelli, told me you might have a job opening there. I don't believe Mrs. Martinelli understood what I said when I called before.”

“Oh, yes. My grandmother doesn't speak very good English.

Hold on a moment and I'll get her back here."

Deloris could hear Mrs. Martinelli and the young person speaking in Italian, and both were raising their voices. After a few minutes more, the young person returned to the phone.

"Hello?"

"Yes."

"My grandmother says that you talked too fast for her to understand. I have her here and I will act as a translator for you."

"Thank you. First, what is your name?

"Oh, my name is Nina."

"Thank you, Nina. I want to know if there is an opening for a waitress job there and if I can apply. Tell her Stella is my friend."

In the background, Deloris could hear Nina relay the message to Mrs. Martinelli and a long response came back. Nina returned to the phone. "Do you have any experience waiting on tables?"

"I've worked as a waitress and a soda jerk in a soda fountain."

Nina relayed the message to her grandmother and then returned. "Yes, she said that you can come by tomorrow afternoon about 2:30, and she will interview you. I'll be there too."

"Thank you. Uh, Gracia, I'll be there. Please tell her thank you for me."

"Ciao."

"Goodbye." Deloris hung up the phone and turned to see Annie walking in the front door. She told Annie the good news.

The next afternoon, Deloris caught the bus to 2225 Indiana Avenue. Standing on the street corner at 22nd and Indiana, she looked around to take in her surroundings. There was a large stone house with a sign outside the basement level, Indiana Gardens. At the top of the house was a widow's walk where, she assumed, a person could watch for any uninvited guests coming to raid the place. Next to it was the Snooker Club that advertised snooker, billiards, pool, and soda pop on the windows in front. Across the street was a grocery store advertising fresh produce. She noticed as she walked up the street that the nearest house in the back of the restaurant was a block away. She could just see the top of it over the tall mound of earth in the backyard of the 2225 address. The entire backyard appeared large, but a tall fence had large wooden slats blocking the view. So, the neighborhood was more residential than commercial and the grocery store, restaurant and Snooker Club were all snuggled in-between homes.

When Deloris walked into the restaurant, there was a warm, welcoming feeling of family and comfort. Inside, she was immediately hit with the aroma of garlic, oregano and tomato sauce again, but there was something else she smelled that she couldn't quite put her finger on. There were a few diners still finishing up their meals and staff rushing around to clean the tables and sweep the floor. There wasn't a bar in sight—only a small counter with two stools—so she felt safe that there wouldn't be a raid on the place.

A young woman greeted her and asked, "Table for one?"

"Oh no, I'm here to see Mrs. Martinelli."

"You must be Deloris," Nina said with a smile.

"Yes, I am."

"I'm Nina. Have a seat over there and I'll get my grandmother."

"Thank you."

When Mrs. Martinelli walked in, she looked at Deloris and started smiling. She was a short, round woman with a face wrinkled from years of memories—good and bad. Then she started talking in Italian too fast to comprehend anything. Deloris stood up to offer her hand in greeting, but looked at Nina and shook her head.

Nina turned to her grandmother and told her to wait until she could translate for her, and the older lady looked back at Deloris, threw her hands up and shook her head.

"I'm sorry. My grandmother says that you look like you should be able to understand her and she thought you would," she explained.

"I studied Latin in high school, but she was talking very fast and I only caught about every third or fourth word."

"I know," Nina laughed. "Sometimes, even I have trouble catching every word she says."

Her grandmother was tugging at her sleeve and indicated that she wanted to know what was said, so Nina turned to her to explain.

Then she said, "Let's have a seat and we will begin the interview. How did you hear of us?"

"Stella, I guess your cousin? She told me about the job," Deloris answered. Mrs. Martinelli had a way of making Deloris feel welcome.

"Oh yes. What kind of experience do you have working in an Italian restaurant?"

"I was working at the Venetian Gardens as a waitress until last weekend when gangsters shot up the place and killed the owner, wounding his wife and brother."

"Oh, I heard about that. You weren't hurt then?"

"No, luckily. I was in the kitchen and the cook pulled me down behind the sink for cover."

"I see." Mrs. Martinelli began tugging on her arm again. "Excuse me," Nina said as she turned to relay the information. Her grandmother shook her head sadly and then said something, then Nina turned back to Deloris. "How long did you work there?"

"I only worked there on weekends for a few weeks."

She translated that for her and then asked, "What were they paying you?"

Deloris told her, but quickly added, "I was hoping to make a little more."

She told her grandmother and then relayed, "She said we could offer you a quarter more per hour."

"I'll take it," Deloris quickly responded. "If you are making a job offer to me, that is."

"We are," Nina said with a smile.

"Wonderful. And I will only be working weekends?"

"Yes. Come back here tomorrow at three o'clock and we'll get you started."

"I'll be here."

<h1 style="text-align:center">Chapter Nineteen
The Shuffle</h1>

That evening, Deloris had a date with Les. On their way to the Aladdin Movie Theater, Deloris saw Sam talking to a man on the street. The man, dressed in a finely tailored suit, looked like the man Franny at the Venetian Gardens told her was Jules Stanford, who operated the Sugarhouse Syndicate. As she walked up to him, she confirmed it was Jules Stanford. She overheard Sam saying, "We got a big game tonight, and I can get you in on the ground floor. Are you in or are you out?"

Before Jules could answer, Deloris interrupted, "Sam! See, I told you I had a boyfriend."

"Oh, hey doll. Yeah, I see that." He smiled, then went back to the Jules. "So, are you in or are you out?"

Taken aback by his less than normal friendly manner, Deloris stood there for a minute before Les pulled her arm to move on. Before she left, she heard Jules respond, "So you say I could make a thousand dollars?"

"He looked a little engrossed in that conversation, which must have been important... I suspect that is why he wasn't more friendly," Les said softly.

Deloris told Les about Sam and the scams he told her about. "He is usually overly friendly. I bet he is setting up another scam." Now she was suspicious of his behavior.

After the movie, Deloris commented, "It's such a beautiful evening. How about we go for a walk?"

"Sounds good to me," Les agreed.

They headed down Belmont toward 18th street and were busy chatting away when Deloris spotted Sam again with the same man.

She nudged Les with her elbow. "Hey, let's follow Sam and see where he goes."

"Are you sure about that? I mean, he could lead us into a den of thieves and we could be robbed," Les answered reluctantly.

"I just want to see for myself what he is doing."

Les relented, and at 18th Street, they saw the two men duck into a store named Little Hollywood. As they approached, they discovered it was a cigar shop.

"Come on, let's go inside," Deloris encouraged.

When they stepped in, the smell of pipe tobacco mixed with the smell of fresh cigars and cigarettes. On the left, they saw a row of glass counters with various brands of cigars in boxes and tins advertising pipe tobacco. Behind the counters were several shelves full of cigar boxes and tin cans full of loose tobacco for both cigarettes and pipes. Packs of Chesterfield, Lucky Strike and Camel cigarettes were also stacked up.

On the right were small tables, sofas, and winged chairs where the patrons could sit and enjoy a conversation over a smoke. In the back of the room was a closed door, but from the sounds emanating from the room, there was some gaming going on.

The man behind the counter looked them up and down and said suspiciously, "May I help you?"

"Oh, my boyfriend here was thinking of taking up pipe smoking and wanted to look at what you have," Deloris improvised. Les looked at her, surprised for a moment, and then nodded his head in agreement.

As the man turned to reach for a pipe, the door opened and in rushed the Kansas City Police, followed by Austin and Big Jim. Deloris mumbled to herself, "Of all people." She quickly turned her back to them.

"EVERYONE GET DOWN ON THE FLOOR, FACE DOWN, WITH YOUR HANDS AND LEGS SPREAD-EAGLE."

Then Austin walked up behind her and grabbed her arm. "Deloris? What are you doing here?!"

She turned to face him but didn't meet his eye. "Oh, uh, Les here was thinking of taking up pipe smoking."

"Uh, huh." It was evident that Austin didn't believe her. Then he followed the rest of the officers into the back room.

All the backroom occupants were handcuffed and brought to the front of the cigar shop. Jules came out, but Sam was nowhere to be seen. Jules started resisting the arrest by jerking his arm out of the grasp of the officer and yelled, "Where is that scum, Sam? I haven't done anything wrong. We just arrived. Do you know who I am?"

"No sir, but we'll find that out when we get to the police station," one officer responded.

"I need to make a phone call to my lawyer," Jules continued.

"Again, sir, you'll get a chance to do that once we book you."

Deloris and Les took advantage of Jules' commotion and slipped into the back room to look around. There were two tables set up for what looked like a poker game, two craps tables, and two other tables covered in felt with a cup and dice on them. Just for fun, Deloris rolled the dice at one table and they did something strange. They rolled to a spot and stopped cold with a jerk. She kneeled down to peer under the table and found a strange contraption. She called Les over to look.

When he picked up the dice, he commented, "These are a little heavier than average dice."

"Look at this," Deloris persisted.

On the table was a humidor with cigars on top of a false bottom that had a magnet inside. Under the table was another magnet with a battery and wires coming from it. The wires came out from the table and were covered with a rug; seeing that, Les pulled the rug back to follow them. They led to the front. Deloris poked her head back through the door to see where the officers were in the arrest process and called Austin to the back room. She showed him the dice, and Les showed him the wires. The group followed the wires to the front counter, where an automobile starter was hidden underneath.

"Ah, what we have here is a crooked dice game," Austin surmised. "But what were you doing in the backroom?"

"I saw a friend come in here and I wanted to talk with him," Deloris said quickly, only explaining their presence in the shop.

"Well, did you speak to him?" Austin asked, hands on his hips.

"No, and I didn't see him come out of the room with the others. So, I thought he was still in here."

"Who is this 'friend'?"

"Oh, just a fellow I met at the Venetian Gardens. I think you should investigate where he went and how he got out of the room?"

Austin rolled his eyes and returned to the backroom to investigate, with Deloris close behind him. They pulled back a curtain to find a door that went out into an alley.

After checking out the alley, Austin came back inside and told Deloris that they had been watching Little Hollywood for some time, waiting for a game night. The call came in that one was in progress, and they raided the place. He told her that this dice game confirmed that the games were rigged to scam rich patrons. But, of course, the scams were seldom reported, because no one wanted to confess to being made a fool. One of the more popular dice games was called Twenty-Six. It all made sense to Deloris now. This is where Sam did his scams or shuffles.

"That's enough. You two better go home before I have to explain to people why you weren't arrested, too," Austin warned, pointing toward the front of the store.

"We're on our way," Les said as he took Deloris's hand and guided her out of the store.

Chapter Twenty

Friday, October 2nd

Deloris showed up at the appointed time the next day at the Indiana Gardens and was greeted by Nina, who gave her a tour and directions on what to do. Walking out the back door, Nina led Deloris through a trellis covered in grapevines that reminded Deloris of the one at the front of the Venetian Gardens. At the end of the trellis was a small mound with a door built into it. She assumed it was a cellar, like the one her mother had up home. Nina explained, "This is where we keep our spices, canned vegetables, and other things we use for the restaurant."

The backyard was huge, and in the back right corner was another hill, but it was larger than the cellar and was covered in decorative flowering vines. Deloris recognized it from seeing it above the fence the day she came for her interview.

"What's that?" Deloris inquired.

"Oh, that's just a little hill in the backyard. As children, we used to run up and down it, playing on the top. We'd get into trouble if we hurt the vines."

To the left was an extensive garden where an older man was picking tomatoes and peppers. Nina introduced him, "Nono, this is Deloris. Remember, we told you she would be here Friday? Deloris, this is my grandfather, Angelo Martinelli, or, as people call him, Angel."

Mr. Martinelli obviously understood English better than his wife, as he smiled and nodded his head. He wiped his hands on his pant leg to brush the dirt off and extended his hand in greeting. "Ciao, welcome," he said, nodding again.

"Thank you. Ciao," Deloris responded hesitantly, not knowing if she should curtsy or bow or just stand. She awkwardly did a small curtsy.

"Come on, there is more to see," Nina urged as they returned to the kitchen.

"Your grandfather certainly has a large garden. What all does he grow there?"

"Let's see." She started counting them off on her fingers, "He has gagootz also known as cucuzza, zucchini, cauliflower, basilico, prezzemolo, Roma tomatoes, artichokes, arugula, broccolini, broccoli rabe, celery, fennel, onions, carrots, Italian green beans, red bell peppers and lacinato kale radicchio. Oh, and also, eggplant and spinach. In the cellar, he also grows portobello mushrooms."

"My goodness. With all of that, he doesn't need to buy much for the restaurant, does he?"

"No, he doesn't. That's the idea," Nina said, beaming.

"What is basilico and prezzemolo?"

"Oh, prezzemolo is parsley and basilico is ... let me see. It is an herb mostly used in our sauces. Basil! That's it. It is basil," Nina said proudly.

"You must need to water a lot?" Deloris observed.

"Oh, we do. Our water hose doesn't reach to the back of the garden, so we use a bucket and a saucepan to carry the water to the vegetables in the back."

In the kitchen, Nina introduced Deloris to her mother.

"Madre, this is Deloris, our new waitress. Deloris, this is my mother, Mary Louisa Martinelli."

"What are you making? It certainly smells good," Deloris said, inhaling deeply.

Smiling, Mary Louisa answered, "This is my sofrito made with celery, onions and carrots. They are the holy trinity of Italian cooking, you know."

At another stove, Mrs. Martinelli was cooking tomato sauce down, adding a pinch of this and a dash of that while she stirred the bubbling concoction.

"I love spaghetti sauce," Deloris said, moving closer to watch the older woman work. Nina's grandmother only smiled back and went back to stirring her sauce. Then she took meatballs out of the oven and started dropping them gently into the sauce with a big spoon so they wouldn't splash.

"We call it sugo, Deloris," Mary Louisa corrected.

"Sugo. Got it. I smell something different in the sugo. What's in it?"

"That's Momma Martinelli's secret ingredient. She doesn't even tell me what it is. The same is with her meatballs. She has a secret ingredient in them, too. Maybe one day she will trust me with the secrets," Mary Louisa laughed.

Nina showed Deloris where to get an apron, order pad, and pencil, and finished the tour. Although Deloris missed the soft music played at the Venetian Gardens, she liked that this was a much quieter and—she felt—safer crowd. Stella surprised her when she walked in and put on an apron.

"What are you doing here? I didn't think you worked here," Deloris exclaimed.

"Oh, I sometimes pitch in, especially when they are shorthanded, and I figured that I'd work tonight to help you until you get accustomed to working here." Stella grinned as she tied her apron strings.

"You certainly are a welcome surprise." With that, they were off taking orders, serving and cleaning up after the customers left.

The next person to walk in surprised Deloris even more: Sam Sloan.

"Sam, what are you doing here?!"

"Hey dollface! I didn't know you worked here."

"I just started tonight—you know, since I can't work at the Venetian Gardens now." She raised an eyebrow and watched his reaction carefully.

"I heard about that. It was a dirty deal. Too bad," Sam said as he shook his head in sadness. "Hey, you know what I want."

Deloris scoffed. "I still have a boyfriend."

"I know. I know. I get it. I have a new squeeze now myself. How about a table in the back and a cup of coffee?"

"You got it. Coming right up," she said as she guided him to a table. "Do you want a menu?"

"Why not?" he said as he took a seat.

When she returned with his coffee, she said, "Say, Sam, you know that your ex-wife was looking for you?"

"Where?" he said as he jumped up, ready to run.

"Not here. At the Venetian Gardens right before the... you know."

"Oh, yeah, that dame is *gagootz*—crazy in the head. I don't know what I ever saw in her." Sam dropped back in his seat. "Actually, I do know. I was pretty drunk that night."

"She said that you stole her mother's brooch."

"I only borrowed it for a little while. I plan to give it back to her soon."

"She says that she's going to kill you when she sees you."

Sam looked around and lowered his voice. "There are several people who want to kill me. She's just one."

"Why are they wanting to kill you?" Deloris pressed.

"Various reasons," he replied with a dismissive wave of his hand. "I hear that Sal Binaggio thinks I ordered the hit on the Venetian Gardens, but I didn't."

"Last night, I saw you when I was with my boyfriend. We saw you later go into the cigar shop, Little Hollywood. Where did you go when it was raided?" Deloris queried.

"You ever hear of the Kansas City Shuffle?" he continued in a hushed tone.

"No."

"Well, that is my skill. You look left and I go right. I shouldn't tell you this, but I feel like I can trust you. Besides, I'm a sucker for a pretty face," he said with a wink.

"You can trust me," Deloris agreed. Intrigued, she urged, "Go on."

"So, I get a chump on the hook and I invite him to this dice game called 26. Only the game is rigged, see. I tell him the game is rigged so that he will win, but it is really rigged so that

I win. I set up the game and have my partner call the police to report the illegal gambling. Once I hear the police enter the place, I grab all the money on the tables and slip out the back door. They call me Slick Sam Sloan, because trouble slips right off me." He stopped to take a sip of coffee.

"I see," Deloris ruminated over what he said.

"That night, I organized a dice game with a chump named Jules Stanford. I didn't know Johnny Lazia's friends were going to be there, too. I tried to stop the raid, but once I saw them, it was too late. Johnny's *goombahs* all got hauled off to jail, but I told Johnny I didn't set his men up for a fall."

After another drink of coffee, Sam continued. "They don't like it when you try to swindle them or move in on their territory. Johnny is a secret partner at Little Hollywood with Harry Brewer. Johnny told me he didn't appreciate me running a shuffle in his cigar shop. I promised him it wouldn't happen again. He was going to kill me if he caught me pulling a scam in his neighborhood again. Then there's Jules Stanford. I took him for over a thousand dollars on the gambling deal. He left his money on the table and I swiped it and took off. Plus, I stole his girlfriend, not that it was hard to do. He doesn't have a brain. If it wasn't for his old man's money, he'd be some sot on the street begging for money. So, he's not happy and says that he is going to teach me a thing or two. I'm not really worried about him. He couldn't fight his way out of a paper bag. Then, of course, there's my ex-wives. They all want to wring my neck."

"Wives? You have more than one?"

"Like I said, I'm a sucker for a pretty face," he winked again and smiled.

"I see that," Deloris said, rolling her eyes. "So, you're a con man? I think I heard that Jules Stanford was a silent partner in the Sugarhouse Syndicate. Isn't that dangerous?"

"That could be, but I don't know that for a fact. The Sugarhouse Syndicate is a pretty powerful group. They may use him because he has lots of money."

"What are you going to do if one of these people shows up here?"

"I'll figure that out when the time comes." Sam handed her the menu and said, "Now, how about you bring me some spaghetti and meatballs, dollface?"

Chapter Twenty-One

The Secret Hideaway

That Saturday afternoon, Deloris found herself in the kitchen alone when there came a knock at the door, giving her a case of déjà vu.

A young man burst through the door with two trays of bread in his arms, "Yeah, I gotcha bread order right here for a C-e-l-i-a M-a-r-i-a-n-i." he spelled out, then showed Deloris the delivery order.

"There must be some mistake," Deloris said. "The owner is Sicilia Martinelli. S I C I L I A not Celia and her last name is Martinelli, not Mariani. Also, we have plenty of bread right here at the moment, see?" And she opened the cabinet to show that they had several dozen loaves of bread stacked up.

"Are you sure about that?" he asked pointedly.

"Yes, I'm..." Deloris stopped herself while she remembered the olive oil. What if they delivered bread instead of olive oil here? "Wait, let me get someone else."

"All right, then."

At that moment, Mary Louisa came into the kitchen and said, "Oh sorry, I was a little late getting here. Just put the bread over there and I'll put it away. Here is the money." Mary Louisa handed him a couple of hundred-dollar bills. Satisfied with the amount, he looked at Deloris, winked, and left.

"You don't really need any bread, see here?" Deloris pointed to the loaves of bread in the pantry.

"I know, dear, but we can't turn down their delivery of bread. It's our insurance policy that we won't run out."

That confirmed she was correct. Thank goodness she figured it out before he left. So, the bread delivery to Indiana Gardens and the olive oil to Venetian Gardens were related. "Insurance policy, huh?" she thought.

"Mary Louisa, what is this insurance policy? The Venetian Gardens had the same thing, but with olive oil."

Speaking in a low tone and taking Deloris aside, she replied, "Oh, honey. It is called the Lug Tax. If we don't take the bread from the Mafioso and pay them, they will torch our place. This ensures that they will protect us from anyone else doing it, too. We don't have a choice if we want to stay in business."

"So, maybe the Venetian Gardens didn't pay the Lug Tax, and that is why they were shot up," Deloris said quietly.

"It is very possible." Mary Louisa nodded sadly. "Any Italian that wants to do business in Kansas City must pay the mob to stay in business or else. It's the unwritten code."

"Oh." Deloris was learning so much from working at these two restaurants, and she couldn't wait to tell Austin and Big Jim.

A little later, she was sent to the cellar to get more mushrooms. As she went out the back door, she noticed Mr. Martinelli at the large mound in the back, where he disappeared behind the vines that covered the mound. She snuck over to investigate closer and saw a door with a grass façade covering it that made it look like it was a part of the hill and virtually impossible to see unless you knew it was there. The vines formed a curtain that could be pulled aside to gain entrance. "These people have secrets," she mumbled to herself, shaking her head and heading back to the cellar.

The next day, Deloris arrived at the Indiana Gardens and started prepping. She was busy cutting up the lettuce when Nina came into the kitchen.

"Hello, Deloris."

"Hi," she answered without looking up.

"Hey, I wanted to ask you if you would be available to work next Sunday night, October 11th, for a special catering event?"

Deloris stopped cutting the lettuce. "Sunday? How late? Because I have to work the next day."

"We start at noon, unloading everything and set-up, with the meal served at 6 p.m. It ends at 9 p.m. and clean-up usually lasts until 10:30 p.m."

"What is the event?"

"It's the annual Christopher Columbus Day Charity Ball that we will celebrate on Sunday instead of Monday, the actual day," Nina explained. "I've called in Stella and some of my other cousins to help with the week's preparations, and serving, too. It will be at the Vacarro Hall at 922 East 5th Street."

"Christopher Columbus Day. That's the day Columbus discovered America, right? Tell me more about it."

"Yes. All Italians in Kansas City and neighboring areas gather to have a daylong celebration of Christopher

Columbus." Nina grabbed a flyer from a bulletin board that hung in the kitchen advertising the event and read the events to Deloris. "At 1:30 p.m., the Verde band leads a parade that starts at Fifth and Charlotte Streets. It winds through the Italian neighborhood and ends at Columbus Square, where there will be a multitude of dignitaries giving speeches. That is scheduled for 3:00 p.m. Then everyone goes home to dress up for the big charity ball at Vacarro Hall. We serve the meal at 6:00 p.m. and dancing follows at 8:30 p.m. with Professor Anthony Bilello's orchestra playing."

Deloris nodded. "I am okay to work, if your Nona wants me to be there."

"Oh, we close the restaurant down for this event every year."

"Well then, I'm available!"

"Peachy! Get ready to strap on your roller-skates, because things are going to get busy."

Deloris continued her prep work and had a busy night serving the customers. She caught Nina later for a clearer idea of the catering job. "Is there anything special I should do to prepare for the event?"

"Well, we will be cooking and baking extra food all week, making different pastas, pastries, and desserts. Oh yes, the desserts are *delizioso*." She kissed her fingertips and raised her hand to the heavens. "We start by making pignoli cookies, almond biscotti, pizzelles, and the outside of cannoli wraps ahead of time. Then we make other desserts and dishes like various pies closer to the day."

It was obvious that Nina was making herself hungry just talking about these foods, but Deloris didn't have a clue what they all were. She would learn, though, and that was exciting.

She asked, "Do you want me to help with that, too?"

"If you're available, we could use an extra hand."

"I can help in the afternoons after I finish my morning shift," Deloris offered.

"Super! I'll tell Nona and Nono that you'll help."

"Do you think I could invite my friend to the ball? My friend Annie is a reporter with the *Post* newspaper and they might like to cover the event."

"You need to ask the man organizing it. His name is Mr. Joe Loscalzo. We have his telephone number here somewhere. Oh, here it is on the flyer."

"Okay, I'll give this information to my friend and see if she can have her boss get her an invitation." Deloris wrote his number on a sheet from her order pad. "Thank you."

After the church rush was over that afternoon, three men came in and asked to speak with Angelo. Deloris went into the kitchen to look for him, but no one had seen him, so she went out to the secret door in the mound and called for him. There still was no answer, so she opened the door and stepped inside. As her eyes adjusted to the dim light, she saw him walking up some rough-cut stairs. He looked up, startled.

"Deloris! What you need?" He stood there with a bottle in one hand and a glass in the other, which he attempted to hide behind his back.

"Uh, there are some men here looking for you. They look important," she answered nervously.

"All right. I'll be up in a minute."

When Angelo entered the restaurant a few minutes later, he greeted the three men and took them next door into the

Snooker Club from the kitchen. The small window in the door that divided the two businesses allowed food to be served through it to the people playing pool or billiards. When the restaurant was closed, the window was closed and locked. But today the window was open, so Deloris stood near it to listen.

"We are adding a case of olive oil to your bread order," one man said.

"I just need a half a case," Mr. Martinelli protested.

"With Venetian Gardens out, we are increasing everyone's order. Got it?"

"Yes."

Deloris went home that night and found Annie in the living room, curled up in a chair and reading. She told her about men who came in to talk with Mr. Martinelli and about the Lug Tax.

"Oh wow. I didn't know about a Lug Tax. I'm going to look into that." Annie grabbed her notepad and wrote it down.

Then Deloris remembered to tell her about the Christopher Columbus event and told her about the different events.

"I'd definitely like to come. Sounds delicious," she said as she licked her lips and rubbed her stomach.

"Well, here is the phone number of the man you need to contact."

"I'll ask my editor to call him tomorrow. Thank you."

"I hope you can come. Where is everybody?" Deloris asked.

"Leota is upstairs with the girls, and I think they are asleep. Edith is in her room. I think she said she was preparing for tomorrow's class lecture and Gracie is out on a date," Annie recounted.

Chapter Twenty-Two
Catering Preparations

All week after her shifts at the switchboard, Deloris helped with the preparations for the Christopher Columbus Charity Ball. On Monday afternoon, Deloris arrived at the restaurant and found five women in the kitchen working: Stella, Nina, Mary Louisa, and Stella's cousins whom Deloris had met at Poppy's Paradise Amusement Park, Rocco and Rossi.

"Hey Stella, it is good to see you," Deloris greeted her friend.

Looking around, she saw Mrs. Martinelli mixing up some batter and giving directions to Mary Louisa to combine ingredients and to mix another type of batter at her station close by. Mary Louisa poured her mixture into a tin mold that Nina put in the oven. The older woman poured her mixture into an apparatus that looked like a waffle iron, and Stella placed it in the oven. Mesmerized, Deloris couldn't help but watch what happened next. After a specified amount of time, Stella took the iron out of the oven and turned it to cook the other side. When the waffly, looking cookie was finished, she emptied the pizzelle iron and started again.

"Sorry, Deloris. I can't stop to talk. I have to keep the irons hot and ready for the next one," Stella said.

"Oh, I understand. Don't let me stop you." Turning to Nina, she asked, "Where do you want me and what are you making?"

"These are almond biscottis. Over there are pignoli

cookies and Stella is baking the pizzelles, one of my favorites. Tomorrow we will make some of my favorite desserts: ciambella, and struffolis." Nina gestured toward the sink. "If you could keep the dishes washed and dried, that would be a great help. Nona doesn't allow anyone outside of the family to know her recipes. She won't allow you to be involved in the various dishes."

Deloris nodded and grabbed an apron from a hook over the door. "Consider it done." She then went to work washing and drying the dirty tin molds, cookie sheets, and spoons.

When the need for more ingredients arose, Nina or Stella retrieved them from the large pantry in the back. Everyone was laughing and talking, and the evening went by quickly. Sometimes the conversation was in English and Mrs. Martinelli looked lost. Then sometimes the conversation was in Italian and Deloris struggled to catch a few words. She could translate a few words here and there that were similar to Latin, but not all of what they said.

Throughout the week, Deloris learned everything they were fixing for the event and picked up some more Italian words and phrases in the process.

The next two afternoons, everyone focused on making more baked goods. Nina said these desserts were also her favorites. Deloris laughed to herself that all desserts appeared to be Nina's favorite. Deloris learned that the desserts on the agenda to be made tonight were almond praline semifreddo with grappa, sfogliaelle ricce, the cannolis' outside pastry shell, and various pies. Deloris learned that the almond praline semifreddo with grappa and poached apricots was Mrs. Martinelli's specialty.

On Thursday, they made various pastas, including agnolotti, ravioli, rigatoni, lasagna noodles, and spaghetti. When Deloris got to the restaurant on Friday, she found everyone already involved and working hard. Mrs. Martinelli made her famous sugo in a large vat that Stella and Nina took turns stirring and her meatballs.

The pastas, except for the lasagna noodles, were still firmly cooked and not mushy—*al dente* Deloris heard Mrs. Martinelli say—with the plan to finish cooking them on Sunday before they were to be served. Baked lasagna sat aside, cooling, with the plan to reheat it on Sunday.

On Saturday afternoon, the remaining desserts that were more fragile were made: tiramisu, chocolate budino with candied walnuts, cannoli fillings, cannoncini, and sweet ricotta pastries. The cannolis and cannoncinis were to be filled with sweet ricotta cheese, whipping cream, powdered sugar; the cannoncinis with Chantilly cream were to be finished on Sunday to ensure their freshness.

As the work slowed, Mrs. Martinelli said something to the group and Deloris looked to Nina for a translation.

Nina chuckled and reported, "She said, 'Thank goodness there is a large kitchen at the hall for us to finish cooking and heating the dishes or we would trample all over each other.'"

Looking around the week's hard work was evident with the kitchen and cooler stocked full of every dish and delicacy imaginable for the event. Everyone looked tired, especially Mrs. Martinelli, but satisfied. The group then focused on getting through the restaurant's evening routine of serving customers and carrying on the restaurant business.

Chapter Twenty-Three
Sam Sloan and The Twins

As fate would have it, Tuesday evening during that week, while Deloris was waiting for the bus to go home, she saw a familiar face coming toward her. Sam Sloan was coming down the street with a woman on his arm. "Is that? Could it be? It is! That's Lilly! So, Sam and Lilly are an item now. That's quick work, Lilly. You were just flirting with Austin not that long ago. Maybe she likes to date two men at once, she thought. I kind of like it," she chuckled to herself.

"Hey, how are you two doing?" she called out.

"Great!" Sam replied as they continued walking toward her. He looked at Lilly and patted her hand that was on his arm. She only smiled, but didn't respond.

"That's not like Lilly," Deloris thought. "She normally talks like a magpie." This time, she tried talking with Lilly directly.

"Lilly, hi. How are you? I guess you don't recognize me. It has only been a couple of weeks since we worked together, but I didn't change that much. Not like you who changed your hair again."

"Oh, hi. Yeah, I'm okay," she answered, looking around.

"Did you get another job?" Deloris asked.

"Yeah, yeah I did."

"Where are you working?"

Sam piped up, "She works at the El Torreon. She's a singer there." He grinned proudly.

"Well, really I am the cigarette girl there, but they let me sing when the main singer is out," she corrected Sam as she squeezed his arm.

"Really? You accomplished all that in two weeks? That's wonderful. I got a job at the Indiana Gardens." Deloris turned to Sam, chattering on. "Hey Sam, may I see that coin of yours again? I was telling a friend about it and I couldn't remember what was on the back."

"Sure doll. Here," and he flipped the coin at Deloris. Lilly gasped while the coin was in the air, but Deloris caught it.

"Shouldn't you be lying low?" Deloris asked him while examining the coin.

"Everything is worked out. It's okay."

"Sam, honey. We need to get going if we are going to catch that movie," Lilly pleaded.

"Oh, yes. Well, here you go, Sam. I don't want to delay you two," Deloris said as she handed the coin back to Sam.

"See ya around, doll," Sam said as he and Lilly continued on their way toward the movies.

The coin was silver, not gold, but Deloris had seen the pileus cap between two daggers on one side, and the bust of Brutus with the correct markings of BRVT IMP and L PLAET CEST on the other side. Sam obviously didn't know that it was very valuable, but it looked like Lilly might have.

That evening, when Deloris got home, she found Annie sitting at the dining room table with a cup of tea and some paper that she had made notes on.

Seeing Deloris's furrowed brow and pursed lips, Annie asked cheerfully, "Hey DeDe. What's wrong?"

Deloris told her about running into Sam and Lilly.

"Sam? The same guy with the coin?"

"That's the one." Then she told her about Lilly's strange reaction, acting like she didn't know her.

"You worked with her at the Venetian Gardens, right? That is strange. Why would she act like that?" Annie tapped her pen on her notes.

"I don't know. It was like we were complete strangers."

"Are you sure it was her?"

"Of course I'm sure, I think..." Deloris paused in thought. "Now I'm not so sure."

"Maybe she just didn't recognize you."

"But we worked closely together even though it was just a short time. How could she forget me so quickly? Then when I asked to see the coin, Sam tossed it to me and she almost had a heart attack. She gasped and held her breath. Something is up and I intend to find out what it is."

On Wednesday night, when Deloris and Leon went on a date to the movies, Deloris was surprised to see Austin there with Lilly, outside the theater.

"Hey Austin," she said as they approached.

Austin looked like he wanted to run in the opposite direction, but knew he was caught and stood his ground. "Oh, hi DeDe. What are you doing here?"

Lilly interrupted, "DeDe, how are you? I've missed seeing you."

It was definitely the Lilly that Deloris worked with at the Venetian Gardens, and she was acting just like she hadn't seen her with Sam just the day before. "Very strange," Deloris thought.

"Hello Lilly. I've missed seeing you too, but I just saw you yesterday."

Lilly laughed. "Oh, that was probably my sister, Tilly."

"I didn't know you had a twin sister. That's making perfect sense now," Deloris said, relieved. "She should have told me that. I thought you were high-hatting me and two-timing my friend Austin here."

"Oh no, I wouldn't do that to you, Deloris, and I definitely wouldn't do that to this good-looking gent," she said, as she smiled coyly at Austin and squeezed his hand.

Austin turned a light pink color. He cleared his throat before repeating more forcefully, "What are you doing here, DeDe?"

"Leon and I are planning to see William Powell in *The Road to Singapore*," Deloris said as she grabbed Leon's arm and he grinned. "What are you doing here?"

Lilly piped up again, "We are planning to see the same movie. We should go together and sit next to each other."

"Yes, let's do that," Deloris agreed.

Austin grimaced, and Deloris knew he was uncomfortable. She beamed, knowing that he was thinking about all the teasing that she and Big Jim were going to expose him to later; he would never hear the end of this. And that is exactly what she planned to do.

Chapter Twenty-Four

Another Raid

Deloris was in the kitchen drying the dishes and silverware after a busy Friday night at Indiana Gardens. She noticed that the small window that separated the restaurant's kitchen from the Snooker Club was open. She could see Angelo and Sicilia, Mr. and Mrs. Martinelli sitting on stools in the club talking, and he was having a glass of what she was certain was whiskey. The underground cave behind the restaurant undoubtedly held the remainder of the stash.

Suddenly, the Martinellis both jumped up when they saw Deloris through the window. Angelo grabbed the bottle of spirits and quickly exited the Snooker Club into the kitchen and out its back door. She watched him run to the back cave, where she assumed he would slip through the door under the vines. Sicilia headed to the door that connected the two businesses and closed the window before entering the kitchen. Mrs. Martinelli stood behind Deloris to see if the window was in her line of vision. She knew Deloris had probably seen what happened and said, "You see?"

"No, no. I wasn't watching," Deloris quickly replied.

"Okay, okay," and she gestured for Deloris to follow her. "You come."

Deloris followed her into the dining room, where Nina was wiping some tables and chairs off.

"What's going on?" Nina said, looking up from her work.

"I accidentally saw something I don't think your grandparents wanted me to see."

"Oh."

Then her grandmother started saying a barrage of things to her in Italian. "Nona, Nona, slow down. *Rallentare*," she said and held up her hands. Then her grandmother stopped and repeated what she said a little slower, enough that Deloris could understand some of what she said.

Turning to Deloris, Nina said, "They are worried that you will go to the police and tell them about the alcohol."

"No, I would never do that," she said quickly, holding up her hands. "I like your grandparents. What they are doing is their business, not mine to tell. You should know that I also saw your grandfather's secret hideaway with what I assume is a still in the back, and I haven't told anyone about it."

Nina relayed the message to her grandmother, who became even more upset. Nina told her more, and she breathed a sigh of relief.

"You see," Nina turned back to Deloris, "Years ago, the government men raided my grandfather's business next door, looking for alcohol. He had stashed it in the time-locked safe. In a former use, this building was a bank. Anyway, he turned the dial to ensure that it locked. He thought the officers couldn't open it to find his whiskey, but they could smell it on his breath. They saw the glass he was using and picked it up. He forgot to rinse out the glass, you see. They took him and the glass to the police station. When they put a little water in the glass, they could get enough liquid to test it for alcohol. He went to jail for a year and a half."

As if on cue, Angelo came back inside and joined the three women. "Deloris, I've worked hard to build up these two businesses," he said.

"I know, Mr. Martinelli, and I won't do anything to destroy them. I promise." Deloris put her hand over her heart.

Satisfied, he turned toward his wife and said something to her in Italian, then he turned back to Deloris and Nina. "You girls can go back to what you were doing now."

Deloris resumed washing dishes in the kitchen, helping Mrs. Martinelli, when suddenly the front door to the restaurant flung open. Deloris peeked through the service window to see the same five fellows that raided the Venetian Gardens restaurant walk into the Indiana Gardens. Nina froze in mid-motion, wiping a table down.

Shocked, Deloris said under her breath, "Oh Lord. I need to get out of here." She rushed to the back of the restaurant and hid behind the big cooler. Mrs. Martinelli walked out to join her husband, and Deloris could hear their conversation clearly.

"Hello officers, what can I do for you?" Deloris heard Angelo say in English, more broken than she had heard him use before.

"We heard you were gambling next door," Agent Boyle accused him.

"No officers, I wouldn't do that. It's illegal." Angelo shook his head and then continued, "No gambling allowed in there. We just have simple games like pool, billiards, and shuffleboard. Oh, and I have a new bocce ball court in the side yard. Let me show it to you. I just got it installed." Turning, Angelo attempted to lead them out the backdoor, and Deloris squeezed her body closer to the wall, but the officers didn't budge. One of them picked up a glass and took a sniff. Angelo was probably having flashbacks.

"You selling illegal hooch, too?" Boyle demanded.

"No, Officer. I just took some medicine. Alcohol for medicinal purposes is allowed, you know. I have bursitis in my knees and the doctor prescribed that I take a shot of whiskey three times a day. I don't sell liquor in here. See, look here behind the bar. All we have is coffee, tea, seltzer water, and soda pop."

Just then, Mary Louisa opened the back door, returning from dumping some vegetable trimmings on the garden. She found Deloris crouched down in the corner beside the cooler. Deloris put her finger up to her lips to say, "Quiet," and Mary Louisa nodded. She peeked through the service window and groaned. When the officers came into the kitchen, Mary Louisa stood in front of Deloris to hide her. After a thorough search of both the billiards room and the restaurant, the federal agents returned to the dining room where Angelo and Sicilia waited for them.

Unable to find any evidence of more alcohol than Mr. Martinelli was allowed for medicinal purposes, or any signs of gambling, the officers got ready to leave.

"If we hear of you selling alcohol or gambling, we will take you in for more questioning," Boyle warned, wagging a finger at Angelo.

"Yes, officer. I promise you won't hear of anything like that. I don't know who would have told you such a thing."

"Okay, see that we don't." Saying that, Special Agent Jerome Boyle and his agents left.

As the door shut behind them, Angelo said, "That was a close one." Mrs. Martinelli seized his arm and dragged him through the kitchen and out the back of the restaurant, where Deloris could hear her screaming at him in Italian. She could easily figure out that Mrs. Martinelli didn't like her husband selling illegal whiskey even if it was only to *famiglia*—family. It was too *rischiosa*, she heard her say. "So, she thinks it is too risky," Deloris translated and understood why Mrs. Martinelli was afraid that they would get caught and lose both businesses and their livelihood.

When the Martinellis returned, Angelo hung his head and continued into the Snooker Club.

As Nina entered the kitchen, Deloris said, "I guess I had better get home now that I am done cleaning. This has been an exciting day."

"Yeah, me too." Nina took her apron off and hung it on the door.

Chapter Twenty-Five

Christopher Columbus Charity Ball
(October 11, 1931)

On Sunday morning, Deloris arrived at Indiana Gardens to find several people already loading their cars, wagons, and trucks to take the food almost twenty blocks to Vacarro Hall. When the last truck was full, she caught a ride with Nina and Stella in Stella's car and they were off. At Vacarro Hall, the ballroom and kitchen were upstairs. Downstairs was the soda pop facility, with the company offices, a small conference room, and restrooms. Deloris, Stella and Nina lugged big trays of desserts and breads upstairs where they found Mrs. Martinelli directing traffic and instructing everyone where to put the various dishes, desserts and breads. In the kitchen, more workers were getting the silverware, dishes, and glasses wiped off and placing them on a cart with napkins to take out to the tables. Everyone was rushing around in different directions.

Deloris put on her serving apron and started putting food on the big table in the main area. At five-thirty, she grabbed a serving dish full of meatballs in the sugo to put out on the table next to the spaghetti.

"Hey DeDe, this is great," Annie said as she grabbed a small meatball from a platter that Deloris had just placed on the table.

"I'm glad you could get an invitation to the ball," Deloris said over her shoulder as she headed back to the kitchen to get bread. On her way, she saw a familiar face sitting in a corner of the room. Sam Sloan twirled the coin in-between his fingers and looked up.

"Hey doll, are you working here too?"

"I am for tonight. What are you doing here, Sam?"

"I came with my latest squeeze. See, you snooze you lose," he said as he motioned to his body, inferring that Deloris missed out on dating him, a real specimen of a man.

Deloris smiled and shook her head. "I'm sure that she will make you happier than I would." As she turned to walk away, he caught her arm.

"Hey doll, I need to ask you for a favor," he said in a low voice.

"What's that?"

"I may need to make a quick exit or find a hiding place later. I heard that someone may come to this event that I don't want to see."

"Which one is it this time, Sam? The butcher, the baker, or the candlestick maker?"

"Very funny, ha-ha," Sam winced. "But can you help me with a distraction if I need one to escape?"

"Why don't you just leave now?"

"I can't. I rode with my girlfriend."

Needing to get back to work, Deloris huffed, "Why can't she leave?"

"She's part of the entertainment tonight."

"Okay, I'll see what I can do."

Later that evening, when she got a minor break, Deloris ran downstairs to the ladies' room. On her way, she ran into Connie and Sal Binaggio climbing the stairs to the ballroom on the second floor.

She stopped in her tracks. "Connie, is that you?"

"Oh, hi Deloris. Yes, it's me. My friends encouraged me to make some changes to myself. Do you like it?" Connie patted her short, blonde, curly hair mimicking the new starlet, Jean Harlow. The long dark blue gown with the lace cape she wore accentuated her new hairstyle and covered the bandage on her shoulder.

"You look stunning. I am so happy to see you. How are you doing?" Deloris asked.

"I'm doing okay. My friends also told me I should go ahead and come to this event. It is one that Nino and I always attended, and I wanted to be here to show our support." She smiled weakly and she and her brother-in-law continued up the stairs.

Continuing on her way to the restroom, Deloris noticed that the door next to it was cracked slightly open. As she neared it, a voice from behind the door said, "Psst, hey doll. Dollface! Psst, over here. I need your help."

Walking over to the door, Deloris hissed, "Sam! What are you doing in there?" She peeked inside and saw that he obviously broke into the manager's office.

"You gotta help me."

Deloris glanced around, then slipped into the room. "Which one are you hiding from here? I thought you had everything worked out?"

"I saw that Sal Binaggio, you know from Venetian Gardens, is here, and I think Connie is with him. Why oh why is Sal here?" He shook his head and continued with panic rising in his voice, "Then I saw Johnny Lazia and his goons walk in with my ex-wife Isabel. Word is out that Johnny is looking for me. He heard I was organizing another game, but that's false! So, I've got the Mafia after me again. That's when I dashed down here. I need you to hurry and get Tilly for me. She can help me escape in her car, or at least give me the keys."

"Tilly?"

"Yeah, she's singing upstairs. You remember. You met her with me downtown that day? I came with her and I need her to get me out of here without anyone seeing me."

"Okay, but I need to do something first," Deloris said.

"Hurry!"

She tiptoed back out of the office and went next door. From the restroom, Deloris could hear Sam talking to someone; it was a woman's voice, and she assumed it was Tilly. When she exited the restroom, she saw a woman with short, curly, blonde hair and wearing a long flowing gown stealthily slipping out the back door of the building. Deloris assumed it was Tilly checking to see if the coast was clear for Sam to come out of hiding, but when she went back up to the ballroom, Tilly was just finishing a song. Confused, Deloris knew Lilly was on a date with Austin, so it couldn't have been her... although the view of the woman from behind looked like her. It was probably one of the other women here, but why did she sneak out the back door? There were several in attendance—including Connie now—with short, curly, blonde hair and a shapely figure. Strangely enough, most of them were wearing blue or dark-colored gowns. Deloris walked to the edge of the stage and motioned to Tilly, who was also wearing a long flowing dark blue gown, to come to her.

She pulled her aside and whispered in her ear, "Hey, Sam said he needs you to help him get out of here."

"Where is he?"

"Here, I'll take you to him." The two women slipped through the crowd. As they cautiously went down the stairs, Deloris turned to Tilly and said, "It's crazy, but I thought I saw you going out the backdoor a minute ago. It must have been someone else, unless your sister is in two places at once," she laughed.

Tilly replied, "Well, as you saw, I was singing. It wasn't me and my sister is on a date. There are several women here that look like me, I noticed."

"I know, you're right. It's crazy how many do look like you."

Deloris stopped on the stairs and looked around at the crowd. She saw Johnny Lazia, his wife and bodyguards sitting in front of the big picture window. At the same time, Sam's ex-wife, Alice, with her brother and two other men were walking up the main stairs and entering the ballroom. "So, it must not have been Alice who scared Sam into hiding since she is just arriving," Deloris thought. At the door to the office, Deloris knocked lightly, but there wasn't a sound, so she eased the door open. There, lying face down on the floor with a knife stuck in his neck, was Sam!

Tilly screamed and Deloris exclaimed, "Oh my God! No, it can't be! I just talked with him!" She rushed over to him to examine the body and feel for a pulse on his neck. Shaking her head, she moaned, "Oh Sam, what did you get yourself into?!"

Having heard Tilly's scream, several people came running downstairs to see what was going on.

Deloris yelled, "We need to call the police!" When she turned, there was Annie with her camera in hand snapping pictures. "She must be in a state of shock," Deloris thought to herself, "if she doesn't realize the gravity of the situation and is still taking pictures." Hearing the word "police," several people hurried out the backdoor to avoid their arrival.

Stella ran in next, saw the body, and gasped. Then she grabbed the phone on the desk to call the police.

Ten minutes later, Big Jim showed up with another detective and several police officers. "Deloris?! You always seem to be in the wrong place at the wrong time. Where is the body?"

"Here, I'll show you," Deloris offered.

As they headed toward the office, she said, "I guess Austin is still on his date and missing all of this fun."

"Yep, he seems to be infatuated."

"The body's in here," Deloris said as she opened the door. "I closed the door to keep the room secure for you."

"Thank you." Big Jim kneeled by the body. "Do you know who the victim is?"

"Yes, his name is Sam Sloan. I talked with him just before he died."

"The Sam Sloan we've been searching for?"

"One and the same," Deloris confirmed. "Tilly and I walked in and found him like this." At that, Deloris noticed Tilly was nowhere to be seen.

"Where is this Tilly?" Big Jim asked.

"I, I don't know. She must be here somewhere."

"What does she look like? I'll have the officers search for her."

"She's about my height with blonde hair cut in a curly bob. She is wearing a sleeveless, dark blue sequined gown."

Someone from the crowd that was left said, "I saw her leave over there," and they pointed to the back door.

"I guess she must have left when several others left when they heard you were coming," Deloris said with a shrug.

"I see." Big Jim turned to the people gathered outside. "Is there anyone else here who knows the victim or saw anything suspicious?"

Everyone shook their heads and started to tiptoe away one by one. He then noticed Annie standing there with her camera. "Have you been taking pictures here?"

"Yes," she replied, tightening her grip on her camera.

"Did you see anything suspicious upstairs?"

"Not that I can remember. It was a lovely affair, and I was enjoying myself too much to notice."

"I will need your camera film, then."

"Okay." She started rewinding her film and then went to a dark corner to open the back and take it out of the camera. Before she handed the film to Big Jim, she said, "Can't I snag a few pictures for the newspaper first?"

"I trust you'll give it to me when you finish, so, all right."

"Thank you."

Turning to the other police officers, Big Jim continued. "Finish up here, fellows, and dust for prints. Be sure to look around more closely for anything else that looks out of place that you may find." Pointing to Deloris, he said, "I'll need you to go down to the police station to make a statement. Okay?"

"Yes. I just need to finish helping clean up here."

"We'll bring you back to help, but I need for you to go with me now to get a statement while everything is still fresh in your mind."

"Okay, then I just need to tell someone where I will be."

At the police station, Big Jim asked Deloris to wait in the interrogation room. She'd been here before and wondered if anyone would be listening from the women's restroom next door. She smiled to herself.

Big Jim came in with a pad of paper and sat down. "Okay, Deloris, tell me what you know about this and how you know the victim."

"As I said before, his name is Sam Sloan, also known as 'Slick Sam' Sloan. He is a grifter, a conman, and he told me he organized poker and dice games. You were in on raiding one recently at the Little Hollywood Cigar Shop. Austin may have told you that I asked where Sam was?"

"Oh, yeah." Big Jim said. He mentioned him.

"He got away, but you arrested some of the organized crime guys in the sweep. They blamed him, he said. So, he was watching out for them."

"Okay," Big Jim wrote the information down in his notepad.

"Oh, and then there was Sal Binaggio and Connie Binaggio."

"Binaggio, why is that familiar?"

"Connie owned the Venetian Gardens restaurant that was shot up two weeks ago and her husband was killed."

"Oh yeah, I knew that name was familiar. I've had a lot of crimes to investigate since that one, unfortunately. They were there, too?"

"Yes, and Sam was deathly afraid of Sal Binaggio. He couldn't understand why he was here tonight. When Sal walked in, I assume that's when Sam ran downstairs to hide."

"Why was Sam afraid of Sal?"

"Because Nino, Sal's brother, and Sam had an argument just a short time before the gangland attack. Sal blamed Sam for the hit that killed his brother. He believed Sam had set up the hit after the argument and was after him. You remember him saying that at the time, right?"

"Do you know why Sam and Nino argued?"

"I think it had something to do with Sam's ex-wives coming into the restaurant and disturbing the diners."

Big Jim made another note in his notepad. "Okay, anything else?"

"To top everything off, I saw Sam's ex-wife, Alice, come in right before Tilly and I came back downstairs to help Sam get out. She threatened to kill Sam if she ever caught him because he stole her mother's brooch. Sam said he only borrowed it. I guess she or her brother, Antonio Messino, could have killed him, then walked around the building to the front and look like they just arrived. Oh, and then Sam told me that Julius Stanford was after him because he stole his girlfriend and a thousand dollars."

Big Jim's eyebrows jumped. "*The* Julius Stanford?"

"No, I meant Jules Stanford, the son."

"That's a lot of suspects, but stealing one's girlfriend hardly seems like a motive to kill someone." Big Jim leaned back in his chair.

"I know, but remember, he also stole money from Jules. That raid at Little Hollywood where the gangsters were arrested and prevented the game from continuing; he was there. Sam took all the money on the table, including his, and left Jules holding the bag, so to speak. I don't know why Sam was at the charity ball, but he told me it was because his girlfriend, Tilly, was singing. I guess she wanted him here for moral support."

"Tilly again. Do you know Tilly's last name?"

"I assume it's the same as her sister, Lilly Ross."

Big Jim's jaw dropped a little.

"Yes, that Lilly Ross," Deloris confirmed before he asked. "Anyway, Tilly is the only one with a rock-solid alibi; she was singing on the stage." Deloris sighed. "Oh, one more thing. Sam had a valuable coin. Did you find any coins on or around his body that looked old? I am almost certain it was valuable."

Big Jim shook his head. "No, we didn't see it, but we will look for it when the coroner brings us his effects. All right, these are some good leads, Deloris. Thank you. I'll get an officer to take you back to Vacarro Hall."

"Thank you."

When Deloris got back, she found that the only folks left in the building were the clean-up crew. She saw Mrs. Martinelli sitting down in a corner crying while everyone else was working, including Mr. Martinelli. Stella sidled up to her and asked, "This was a pretty exciting night, huh? Where did you go?"

"Because Tilly and I found the body, I had to go down to the police station to give a statement. What do I need to do here?"

"Well, everyone left shortly after the police left. Those that were still here helped, and we got an early start on cleaning up," she gave a half-hearted little smile.

Watching Mrs. Martinelli, Deloris asked, "What's wrong with your grandmother?"

"Nona? Oh, she's upset that we spent all this time working on the desserts and they were hardly touched," Stella shrugged. "Oh, and of course, that someone killed Sam."

"It is a shame," Deloris said sadly. "Did you know Sam or Tilly?"

"Not really. Sam has, um, had a reputation of someone to stay away from. I've seen him in the restaurant once or twice. Who is Tilly?"

"Tilly was the singer."

"Oh, then no. I don't know her at all. Mr. Loscalzo probably hired her."

By the time Deloris got home that night, she was exhausted. What a night. She didn't even have the energy to tell everyone at the boarding house about what happened. However, when she opened the door, Annie, who had gotten home before her, had obviously shared the news, because Thelma jumped up the minute she saw Deloris. Gracie, Edith, and Annie rushed her, too, but Thelma got to her first. Even Leota looked interested in hearing the story.

"What happened? Are you alright?" Thelma asked, grabbing Deloris's hands.

She nodded. "I'm okay. Just a little shaken up having just talked with him, the victim, that is, one minute and finding him dead the next." Deloris shuddered. "Maybe I am getting more steeled to finding and seeing dead bodies. I'm sure Annie told you everything that I could tell you, but right now I am absolutely exhausted and I need to get up and go to work in the morning. So please forgive me if I go to bed."

"Of course," was the reply from everyone, but with an air of disenchantment. She hated to disappoint them, but she needed to head up to her room and get some sleep. As she lay in bed, she went over in her mind everything that had happened. Then she realized that she forgot to tell Big Jim about the woman she saw leaving by the back stairs when she went to get Tilly for Sam. Well, she'd do that on her first break tomorrow. For tonight, her pillow was calling her name.

Chapter Twenty-Six

The Clues

Monday morning, when Deloris had a break, she ran downstairs to see Big Jim. She hadn't told her co-workers yet about her exciting night. She'd tell them later.

"Hello, Deloris. What can I do for you?" Austin said.

"Where's Big Jim?"

"He took the morning off, not that it's any of your business."

"Oh, well, I remembered something else to tell him, and I had a question."

"You can tell me."

"Okay." Deloris sat across from Austin at his desk. "I wondered if anyone found the coin that Sam had on his person when I last saw him alive."

"No, what coin?"

"I told Big Jim about a coin that Sam twirled between his fingers, and he had it right before he was murdered. I believe it's worth a lot of money and may have been another reason he was murdered, especially if you can't find it."

"Oh, yes, he told me about it," Austin confirmed. "No, we didn't find it, but we'll keep looking."

"I remembered something else that I forgot to tell him last night. I saw a woman slip out the back door about the time that Sam was probably murdered."

"Oh, really?" Austin grabbed a notepad and started writing what Deloris said. "What did she look like?"

"I only saw her from the back. She had short blonde hair, a curvy figure and was wearing a long flowing gown in a dark color, possibly dark blue, dark emerald green or even black, I think. It was dim and I couldn't see the color clearly. I just know that it was a darkly colored gown. It was open at the back with a wide collar and three long straps connecting the collar to the back of the dress. I originally thought it was Tilly, because she looked like her from the back. But it wasn't Tilly, and you were out with Lilly last night, right?"

"Yes, I was. We went to a movie. So, this woman was about Lilly's height and weight?"

"Yes, but that is all I know about her. There were several women at the event with darkly colored gowns and blonde curly hair. It could have been any number of women, from Sam's ex-wife who I saw arrive just after we found the body, to Connie Binaggio, who surprisingly changed her hairstyle and color to blonde, or Johnny Lazia's wife who was also Sam's ex-wife." Deloris blew out a breath in frustration. "I'm sorry that I can't give you more details."

"That's okay. This still helps."

Satisfied, Deloris started to leave and go back to the switchboard, when Carolyn Bechtel, the assistant coroner, walked in. Austin turned back to his desk when he saw Carolyn, which meant that he didn't see Deloris leave. Deloris's curiosity won out, and she slowly walked away and then pretended to drop something and ducked behind a desk so that she could eavesdrop.

"Hello Miss Bechtel, Carolyn?" Austin corrected himself as he lowered his head slightly.

"Yes, hello, Mr. Martin, and you may call me Miss Bechtel," she said in a chilly tone.

Deloris assumed Carolyn knew about Austin dating Lilly, since it was obvious by her attitude that she wasn't happy with him. She wasn't her usual friendly self. It was clear that she liked Austin, but neither one had made the first move to date.

"What have you got?" he said, clearing his throat. "Miss Bechtel?"

With strictly business-like mannerisms, she responded, "This is about the stabbing victim from last night. Just as we thought, the victim's cause of death was a knife wound in the neck where it nicked an artery. The victim bled out. He died about eight o'clock. Oh, and here are his personal effects."

At that, Deloris stood up from her hiding spot to see Carolyn hand Austin a box. She tried to peek over his shoulder and could just make out that Sam's suit jacket was on top.

"Thank you, Miss Bechtel."

Carolyn vacillated, as if she wanted to say something.

Austin said, "Is there anything else?"

She shook her head, looked over his shoulder at Deloris, and turned to walk away. He watched as she left, then turned around to come face to face with Deloris, who had been standing directly behind him. He jumped.

"Deloris! You scared me to death. What are you still doing here?"

"She didn't sound happy. I couldn't help but see that Carolyn brought Sam's things in the box there."

Austin moved to block her view. "You need to leave."

"I just want to see if the coin is in there before I leave. Come on, Austin. I can help you, because I knew him and I might see something that you will miss."

He sighed, "Just for a minute."

Austin spread the items out on his desk and Deloris picked up the bloody jacket. She took a sniff or two and recognized a faint smell of perfume. One of Deloris's guilty pleasures was to go to the stores downtown and smell the perfumes. The smell seemed familiar, but she couldn't place it.

"Smell this," she said as she thrust the jacket up to Austin's nose and he jerked his head back quickly in response. "This is not Tilly's perfume. I would expect it to be hers since she was dating Sam. This may be the killer's perfume. Maybe it belongs to the woman I saw slipping out the back door. You should find someone with an acute sense of smell to see if you can find out where it was sold."

"Yes, boss," Austin replied, slightly irritated.

Deloris went through the pockets in both the jacket and the pants. She picked up the shoes and looked closely at the money and keys that Carolyn had put in a small dish. As she started to put the shoes back in the box, something caught her eye. The heel had a line in it. She thought it might be broken and twisted it. It opened to reveal a hidden compartment where a key was hiding.

Holding it up, she said, "I wonder what this is to? It looks like a safe deposit box key."

"Give me that!" Austin said as he grabbed the key from her hand.

"Hey you might not have found it, if I hadn't helped."

"I'm sure we would have. Don't you need to get back to work?"

"Okay, okay. I'm going."

When Deloris arrived back at her station at the switchboard, she found Joyce and Pam in a lively discussion.

"What's going on, guys?"

Pam spoke up first, "Joyce here is upset at a neighbor who parks their car in front of their house, halfway blocking her driveway. I simply said that she should go over and ask them to move it."

"I asked them, and they ignored me," Joyce complained. "I'm going to call the police this time."

"So, ask them again."

"I shouldn't have to ask them again. They should know."

"Apparently, they don't know or they forgot. You just need to remind them before you call the police," Pam insisted.

Before Joyce could respond, the phones started ringing and Deloris welcomed the interruption. She didn't like to see her friends argue.

Chapter Twenty-Seven
The Hunt

As soon as Annie got home that evening, Deloris told her about the safe deposit box key and the perfume, but that they found no coin. That's when the girls decided to do a little investigating themselves.

"Where in the world can the coin be unless the murderer stole it from Sam?" Deloris asked Annie rhetorically.

"That is a possibility. Or it could have dropped somewhere on the floor and rolled under something," Annie mused.

"Good point. I have an idea," Deloris snapped her fingers. "Maybe we should go back to Vacarro Hall and look around for the coin there."

"Isn't it taped off as a crime scene?"

"Yes, so?" Deloris's wicked smile told her plans. "I also need to find out more about the woman I saw slipping out the back door when I came out of the bathroom. How can I go about locating her?"

"Describe her again," Annie requested.

"She was about five foot two, curvy figure with short, blonde, curly hair. But several of the women at the event had short, blonde curly hair, because of Jean Harlow, I guess." Deloris tapped her cheek thoughtfully. "Even Joe Lazia's wife could fit this description. She wore a dark-green colored evening gown that I believe was satin."

"That isn't much to go on. Let's see. We could try to track down the dress?"

"Yes, that is an excellent idea! After we go to the dress shops this week, we can go to Vacarro Hall on Sunday when most of the surrounding buildings are vacant."

Deloris took a sheet from Annie's notebook to sketch the dress and surprised herself at how good it looked. Then she duplicated it for Annie to take. They wrote down all the dress shops and stores that sold dresses and evening apparel. Finishing, they headed to Petticoat Lane, where most of the stores were located. They split up. Annie was to go to Crane's Dress Shop, Diamond Brothers, Emery Bird Thayer, Jones, Maggy Rouff's Dress Shop, and Woolf Brothers. Deloris went to Berksons, Dame Fashion, Edna Marie Dunn's Dress Shop, Elite Dress Shop, Harzfeld's, Pecks and Rothschild's.

After having no luck at the first five shops and stores, Deloris entered Rothschild's. Inside the store, three young women approached Deloris, giving spritzes of various perfumes to all the customers as she walked inside. She smelled all three of the scents, but didn't recognize any of them to be the one on Sam's jacket. However, she allowed one young woman to give her a spritz of a French perfume she liked — "only in the interest of research, of course," she thought to herself and smiled. Going up to the second floor, she found the better-made dresses with a dressmaker's shop in the back. Looking around, she waited for someone to come to the front of the shop to help her. Much to her surprise, Tilly walked out of the back room.

"Tilly! I didn't know you worked here."

"Yes. I sing on weekend evenings at the El Torreon, but I work here throughout the week," she explained.

"Oh, that's right. I believe Lilly mentioned that to me when she told me about you. How nice that you get to work here. Where did you run off to at the Vacarro?"

Tilly dropped the hanger she was carrying and bent down to pick it up before answering, "I, uh, I was afraid someone was going to stab me too because I was with Sam. Lilly told me about when the G-men raided the Venetian Gardens and hauled you all off down to their headquarters. I was upset and didn't want to go through any interrogation."

"That makes sense. I sure didn't like that either," Deloris agreed. "Well, I wonder if you can help me. I'm trying to find out where this dress was made," she showed Tilly her drawing of the dress, "and to whom it was sold?"

Tilly took the drawing. "I believe that is our Vionnet dress. One of our most popular dresses. Let me look in our book." She went behind a counter and ran her finger down a few pages. "It looks like we sold twenty-five dresses of several colors that basically look like your drawing in the past six months."

Disappointed, Deloris responded, "I see. How about in the last two months?"

"That narrows it down to eleven. Myself being one. The one you saw me wearing that night was borrowed from the shop," Tilly offered.

"Any chance I can get a copy of the women's names who purchased the dresses?"

"No, I'm sorry. I can't do that." Tilly eyed Deloris as she shut the book. "Why do you want to know?"

"I was thinking of having a dress made and I wanted to ask them how they liked the dresses and how they fit."

"Oh."

Deloris continued, "What is that perfume you are wearing?"

"It is Ciro's Danger perfume."

"What an odd name for a perfume. You weren't wearing it the night of the charity ball, were you?"

"No. I just purchased this yesterday."

"Does Lilly have a bottle of it?"

"No, but she will probably borrow mine," Tilly said, sounding frustrated at a sister who borrows all of her things.

"So, they sell this perfume here?"

"Oh yes, on the first floor." Tilly paused, narrowing her eyes. "You ask a lot of questions."

Ignoring her comment, Deloris continued, "So, about that dress. Do you think you can help me? I think I want to go ahead and order one."

"Certainly. If you are interested in purchasing one, they were $99.50, but on sale today at $22.50. Let me get my tape measure and pen. I'll be right back."

It surprised Deloris to see that she left the book behind when she went to the back room. "It couldn't hurt to just take a peek," she thought. She casually opened the book and took a glance at the August and September sales. Three names that stood out from the rest were Mrs. Joe Lazia, Mrs. Sam Sloan, and Mrs. Nino Binaggio. Connie! Deloris couldn't believe that Connie could have murdered Sam. She refused to believe that. Also, it interested Deloris that Alice was still using Sam's name, even though they were divorced. Then she thought that the woman with Joe Lazia was his girlfriend, but apparently, she was his wife. Deloris heard footsteps and quickly closed the book and moved to look around the shop.

Tilly came back with her measuring tape and Deloris said, "Oh Tilly, I am so sorry to have bothered you. I just remembered that I promised to meet a friend, and I need to leave. Again, I am sorry."

Looking puzzled and a little suspicious, Tilly put the measuring tape on a table next to the book and watched as Deloris turned and walked away. Outside, Deloris saw Annie coming down the street toward her.

"Did you have any luck?" Annie asked.

"I did!" Deloris answered triumphantly. "How about you?"

"No, but I found some dresses that I'd like to go back and buy."

"I know. Me too," Deloris laughed.

"So, what did you learn?"

"I learned Tilly now wears the same perfume that I smelled on Sam's coat, but she claims that she just bought it. The name is Danger by Ciro. Then I learned that Sam's ex-wife, Alice, Connie Binaggio and Johnny Lazia's wife, Isabel, who is another of Sam's ex-wives, all bought the same dress—the Vionnet, as did Tilly. Well, Tilly borrowed the dress. Anyway, Rothschild's sold eleven of them in various colors over the past two months."

"Wait, Tilly?"

"Oh yes, I found her."

"Were all the dresses dark colors?"

"I didn't get to see that. Tilly came back too soon," Doris lamented.

"Came back?"

"Well, I took a peek in her sales book when she went to the back room to get a tape measure."

"A tape measure?"

"Yes, I told her that I was interested in having a dress made. She became a little suspicious of me asking so many questions, and I didn't want to tip my hand, in case she told any of the women that I was asking. So, I pretended to be shopping for a dress."

Laughing, Annie said, "Okay."

"I did find it suspicious that the three women who had a motive to kill Sam all bought the same dresses at Rothschild's. And Tilly was wearing the perfume I smelled on Sam's jacket. We now know the name of the perfume, at least."

"Well, that isn't unusual since she was dating Sam," Annie countered.

"No, but she said that she just bought it, and I didn't smell it on her the night of the ball."

"What was the perfume name, again?"

"Danger by Ciro."

"Did you check at the perfume counter to see who purchased the perfume?"

"No, I was just excited about the dresses. I forgot. Let's go back inside and ask."

Waving off the perfume sample girls explaining that she

already had a spritz, Deloris headed to the perfume counter. Annie, on the other hand, took a free spritz and came to the counter with her new scent.

"Oh, that smells lovely," Deloris complimented.

"I liked your perfume, so I decided to treat myself to one too," Annie grinned.

"May I help you?" the woman behind the counter asked.

"Yes, I was wondering if you have any Danger by Ciro?"

"Oh, I am sorry, but we sold the last bottle this morning. We should have it back in stock next week."

"That's okay. Would you be able to tell me who purchased the perfume in the last two months?"

The woman frowned. "I'm sorry, but I can't give out my customers' names."

"I understand."

Back outside, Deloris said, "I expected that to be a waste of time. I will tell Big Jim and Austin and ask them to check it out. They can also find out about the color of the dresses that were sold."

Satisfied with their accomplishments, the girls headed home and started preparing supper.

Chapter Twenty-Eight
Vacarro Hall

The following Sunday, Deloris and Annie caught a bus to Vacarro Hall and circled the building, looking for a way to get inside since all of the doors were locked, including the back door everyone exited through the night of the murder. There was a fire escape ladder on the backside of the building, but it was higher up than Deloris or Annie's reach. It led to a door with two windows on each side and a small platform with a railing around it on the second floor. Annie gave Deloris a boost to the ladder, and Deloris climbed up to the balcony to see if she could find a window or door open. She tried the door first, and of course, it was locked.

"Any luck?" Annie asked in a soft yell from the ground.

"Not yet," Deloris said back in a stage whisper. The two windows on the left side were both locked tight, but she was in luck: one window on the right was opened slightly, although it wouldn't go up any higher. It was at the edge of the platform. The other window wasn't over the platform at all. She leaned slightly over the railing to check the other window, but was afraid to look down. It didn't budge at all, so she went back to the closer window. To get the right leverage on that window, she stood on a chair that someone left there when they must have been taking a smoke break.

"Be careful!" Annie warned.

Deloris grabbed a nail file from her purse and used it to dig at the edges of the window where paint halfway sealed it.

She finally jimmied the window high enough to allow her to squeeze through the opening. She stood on the chair again and managed to get her body through the window to her waist. She paused for a breath, nervous because if she fell backwards or to the right, the drop to the ground was two stories. If Annie tried to break her fall, she would get hurt, too. Deloris wiggled and pushed until she got her body inside, up to her legs. The floor below the window was about three feet down, but she didn't relish falling on her head. She threw her purse to the side and stretched her arms out in order to put her hands on the floor and break any fall. She stood on her hands briefly until she could get her feet down. Straightening her skirt, she found herself in a small room next to the kitchen, and she ran downstairs to open the back door to let Annie inside. Together, they went to the manager's office, where Sam was murdered. There was a sign on the locked door warning no entrance to the office.

"What'll we do?" Annie asked.

"Let me try this." Deloris took two bobby pins out of her hair. The first one she opened wide to a ninety-degree angle, took the bulbous end off and stuck it in the lock to bend it up slightly. The other pin she stuck in the lock from where the pin was folded and slightly bent it up. She stuck that pin in the lock. She pushed the straight pin against the mechanisms and used the other pin to raise each cylinder in the lock. Then pushed the straight pin under it to prevent the cylinder from dropping back and closing again. She had to wiggle the last one around until it unlocked. "It worked! I wasn't sure it would."

"Where did you learn to do that?" Annie asked incredulously.

"Oh, it's just something I picked up from a book I was

reading," Deloris said with a sly grin.

Inside the room, Deloris looked around to see a chair overturned by the desk and pictures askew. There was still a bloodstain from where Sam lay, but there wasn't much else in the room to see.

Moving behind the desk, she pulled out the drawers. One drawer was stuck and only opened halfway. She reached her hand into it and felt around. She found a slip of paper and pulled it out.

"What is it?"

Deloris examined the slip. "It looks like an order for soda pop."

Handing it to Annie, she then noticed a sliver of paper sticking out of the heat register on the floor. She kneeled down and removed the paper carefully, then took the flashlight that Annie brought and flashed it into the vent.

"What did you find this time?" Annie asked.

"A pawn shop receipt."

"Really? Which pawn shop?" She moved closer to Deloris to read over her shoulder.

"It says Jones Pawn Shop at 13th and Walnut. Okay, let's get out of here before we get caught and try the pawn shop tomorrow."

"Sounds good to me!"

Chapter Twenty-Nine

The Pawn Shop Receipt

Monday at the police station, Deloris decided not to tell Austin and Big Jim what she and Annie had learned the day before until after they went to the pawnshop. That afternoon, she and Annie went to the pawnshop and handed the proprietor, a balding, middle-aged man, the receipt.

"I don't believe I've seen you two in here before," he said with one eyebrow raised, eyeing them up and down.

"You are correct," Annie spoke up. "Our uncle gave this to us and asked us to collect it for him."

Deloris chimed in, "Can you tell us what it is?"

"Let me see," he said as he pulled a book from under the cash register. Scanning the pages, he eventually said, "Looks like it is a diamond brooch. Hocked by a man named Sam Stein on September 25th. Is that your uncle?"

"Yes, yes. That's Uncle Sam," Deloris said, nodding. "How much do we owe you for it?"

"Looks like you owe me $50."

The girls looked at each other. "Oh dear. He didn't give us enough money," Deloris said apologetically. "We need to come back when we get more money. Thank you, Mr. uh..."

"Johnson."

"Mr. Johnson."

When the girls left the shop, they walked down to the bus stop before they said anything to each other in case Mr. Johnson followed them or could hear them.

"What do you think?" Annie asked.

"I think that brooch is the one Sam took from his ex-wife and, for some reason he gave a false name when he hocked it. I think it is time that I go see Big Jim and Austin with all of this."

"I'm coming with you," Annie volunteered.

At the police station, Deloris walked right past the front desk, as was her custom, but Annie held back. "Come on. It's okay. Sergeant Cox here doesn't mind."

"Well, uh," he started, but Deloris pulled Annie along behind her before he could object. She entered the detectives' room, where she saw Big Jim in the captain's office. Austin was standing at the door, but when he saw the girls, he quickly walked toward them.

"What brings you two in here?" he asked.

"We've got information to share with you, but first, you need to request permission or whatever you get,"—Deloris waved her hand dismissively — "so that you can get these things we are going to tell you about."

"What? So, you've been doing my job for me again?"

Big Jim left the office and joined them. "What's up?"

"They want us to get search warrants," Austin replied.

"What?" Big Jim's jaw dropped.

"I was just telling Austin here that you guys need to order

three, uh, search warrants to get information on the Vacarro Hall murder," Deloris explained impatiently.

"Why is that?" Big Jim folded his arms across his chest.

"We tracked down where we think the dress and perfume was sold to the woman, I saw leaving by the back door the night of the murder.

"The perfume?" Big Jim looked at Austin, who shook his head slowly.

Looking at Austin, Deloris said, "Remember, I told you that I smelled perfume on Sam's jacket?"

"Where did you get Sam's jacket to smell it?!" Big Jim looked at Austin again.

"She was there when Miss Bechtel brought me Sam's personal effects and looked through them before I could stop her," he said, glaring at Deloris, who shrugged.

"I see. Go on," Big Jim said with a sigh.

"Okay. So, I believe the dress was sold at Rothschild's. You need a warrant to look at the sales book to see who all bought Vionnet styled dresses there that were of a dark color. I know that Sam's ex-wife, Alice, bought one, Johnny Lazia's wife, who also happens to be another of Sam's ex-wives bought one, and," with a softer voice she added, "Connie Binaggio."

"How do you spell that dress?

"V I O N N ET."

"And how do you know this?" Austin retorted.

"Don't ask," Deloris answered. "Anyway, then you need to get a warrant to find out who bought the perfume by Ciro called Danger in the last few months." From the look on their faces, she said, "I know. How à propos. And then there is the pawnshop."

"Pawnshop?" Austin and Big Jim said in unison.

"Yes, I found a pawn shop receipt and discovered that it is where Sam must have hocked his ex-wife, Alice's brooch that belonged to her mother."

"Where did you find this pawn shop receipt?" Austin asked suspiciously.

"Never mind that, just get the search warrants to find out more information from these three places. Oh, and I think you were looking for Tilly. Well, I found her, too, at Rothschild's, working in the dressmaking shop."

Big Jim looked at Austin and said, "I feel like we just took orders from the captain. How about you?"

"Yeah," Austin said as he sat down behind his desk.

Deloris snapped her fingers. "By the way, did you find anything in the safe deposit box?"

"How does she know about that?" Big Jim asked, exasperated.

"I'm the one who found the key," Deloris replied smugly. "If it wasn't for me, you wouldn't have known about it."

"I believe we would have found it, eventually. You just beat us to it," Austin countered.

"So, what did you find?"

"Might as well tell her, since she will probably find out anyway," Big Jim said ruefully.

Austin sighed. "We found a lot of cash, and a little black book full of names, addresses, characteristics of people, and how much he swindled out of them."

"May I see it?"

"No," they replied in unison.

"Just a peek? You never know what I might see that you won't. Remember, I knew Sam, and you didn't."

Giving up, Big Jim took the little black book out of his desk drawer and handed it to Deloris. She paged through the book, with Annie looking by her side. She thumbed back several pages and started looking at what Sam wrote. Eventually, she found what she thought might be the information on the man who Sam may have taken the coin from.

"Interesting."

"What is it?"

"I think this is the man who Sam got the coin from; his name is Vincent Rossi. Interesting, that's just one letter off from Tilly and Lilly's last name."

"Don't go there," Austin warned.

"Oh, I just thought it was a coincidence. I wasn't implying anything," Deloris said reassuringly. "Neither of them could have stabbed Sam. They are the only ones with rock-solid alibis."

"True."

"We'll check out the information you gave us. Thank you," Big Jim offered.

Feeling proud of their accomplishments, Deloris and Annie

left and went home.

The next day at work, Deloris rushed downstairs as soon as she had a break to see if there was any news from Big Jim and Austin, but found that they were out. She assumed they were following up on what she and Annie had told them the afternoon before, so she took herself to lunch. When she finished, she returned to the police station and found they had returned.

"What did you find out?" she asked eagerly.

"We have the diamond brooch and will bring Alice Sloan in this afternoon to identify it. We have the dress shop and the perfume counters' sales receipt books. We will be bringing in all of the women who bought the dresses and the perfume to question them later too," Austin replied.

"May I see the books?" Deloris asked.

"Why not," Austin agreed.

Deloris opened the book and pointed to a few entries. "Look here, all the dresses were of a dark color. Why did Tilly purchase a bottle of the perfume two months ago when she told me she bought one recently? I doubt she would need another bottle so soon. Maybe Lilly took that one."

Chapter Thirty

The Newspaper

When Deloris got home later that day, she met Annie at the front step, getting home from her work. They found Gracie reading the evening paper in the living room. Annie noticed the newspaper's date and commented, "That's last week's paper. Why aren't you reading tonight's paper?"

"I didn't get a chance to read your article about the murder at the charity ball. I kept this paper up in my room until I could read it, but first, what have you two been up to? We haven't talked lately." Gracie folded the paper and put it in her lap.

"Oh, you know, breaking into second story buildings, interrogating shop clerks, assisting the police with general sleuthing," Annie replied as she and Deloris sat on the couch with Gracie.

"Sounds exciting. Tell me all about it, but first tell me about breaking into buildings? What's that all about?"

Deloris explained in great detail about Vacarro Hall and Annie added the part of Deloris's lock-picking skills. Then they told her about the murder and suspects. When they finished, Gracie exhaled. "You two have all the fun. I need to hang around you more often, so that I can have exciting adventures instead of homework."

"By the way, how are things going for you and Edith?" Annie asked.

"Luckily, no one knows we both live here, and we have kept our distance from each other on campus. I try to limit going to her office with questions and, as you know, we don't talk about it here."

"Sounds like you have it worked out pretty well."

When Deloris and Annie went upstairs to put their purses away, Gracie picked up the paper and resumed reading it. The first page had a picture of the group outside the room where Sam was murdered. The story continued on the sixth page where more pictures from earlier in the evening were shown. Deloris and Annie sat back down next to Gracie on the couch when they returned. Gracie turned to the sixth page and looked at the pictures.

"So, this is Tilly singing here?" she asked, pointing to a picture of her on stage.

"Yes," Annie nodded.

"She looks just like some girls that I went to school with in Sedalia last year. In fact, she looks a lot like them."

"Tilly does have a sister named Lilly," Deloris offered.

"They were triplets."

"Triplets?" Deloris and Annie said in unison.

"Yes, they were identical triplets. Mildred, Lilibeth and Matilda Rossi. Milly, Lilly and Tilly. They were so much fun, always pretending to be each other and confusing everyone in town, and especially our teachers," Grace said with a chuckle.

Deloris and Annie jumped to their feet and looked at each other, then Deloris ran to the phone to call Austin. Gracie watched in amazement at how fast they reacted to her comment.

"Austin, you need to come over here quick. Well, throw some pants and shoes on and get over here," Deloris ordered.

When he arrived, she directed him to have a seat, which he did, forcefully.

"Deloris, I don't appreciate you thinking you can call me up and order me to come running over here anytime you get an idea," he said with a huff.

"This is more than an idea, Austin, and you will appreciate what we have to say."

"We?" He looked around at Gracie, Annie, and back to Deloris. Feeling outnumbered, he relented. "Okay, what have you got?"

"Gracie, you tell him what you told us."

She repeated the conversation about the triplets, and Austin's eyes widened. "Well, I'll be. Can I use the phone?" He grabbed the phone and called Big Jim to come over.

When Big Jim arrived, they sat him down and repeated the whole story. "Unbelievable! and they could have gotten away with it too, if not for you, Gracie." Big Jim smiled at her appreciatively. "We got the warrants and found out that someone named Matilda Rossi actually purchased a dress. Tilly purchased a bottle of the perfume back in September and again this month. Seemed strange that she would purchase two bottles of perfume so close to each other. That put her at the top of our suspect list for a moment, but we couldn't figure out how she did it. Now..."

An understanding crossed Austin's face, and he sat down hard on the sofa. He obviously just realized that he was used and was doubly upset that Lilly could be involved in something nefarious right under his nose. "Was I used for an alibi?" He dropped his head into his hands.

"I'm sorry," Deloris sympathized and put a hand on his shoulder.

Big Jim added, "And the brooch was the one that Sam took from his ex-wife. We confirmed that by bringing her in to identify it today."

Edith arrived home and, looking at everyone's faces, she asked, "What's going on?"

"It looks like we just cracked the murder case!" Deloris crowed. "With Gracie's help."

Big Jim stood up. "I think we need to bring them in for some questioning—all three of them," he said angrily.

"I'm coming with you," Deloris said as she stood and ran upstairs to grab her purse.

Annie, Edith, and Gracie piped up, "Me, too." Then Annie added, "Grab my purse too, please."

Chapter Thirty-One

The Escape

Austin complained at first, but then agreed that Gracie, Deloris, and Annie might come in handy. Big Jim looked at Edith and knew he didn't have a leg to stand on with stopping her from coming, too. They went to the girls' apartment and knocked, but there was no answer. Their knocking woke the landlady, who came out of her apartment bleary-eyed with pin curls in her hair, a hairnet covering them and wearing a nightgown covered with a robe. She quickly tied the belt on her robe and held the gap at the top with her hand. She told them that the girls should be in their apartment as far as she knew. Big Jim and Austin showed her their badges and she let them in to look.

It was apparent that the girls left in a hurry because everything looked tossed, but the bed was still made, although the mattress was askew. Looking under the bed, Deloris spotted something stuck to the underside of the bedsprings hanging down. She leaned down further to pick it up.

"Don't touch anything!" Austin reprimanded. "Fingerprints, remember."

"Touché. Well-played." She put on a glove and grabbed it. "I was just going to get this." She handed him a piece of paper that was a receipt for mailing a package to Sedalia, Missouri, with a "Will Call" on it. "I wonder what they mailed in that package," she mused.

"We'll call and have the police in Sedalia pick it up for us," Austin said.

"Sedalia is big enough to have a police force?" Gracie commented.

"Or the Sheriff's Office. Good catch," Big Jim corrected, smiling at her.

With nothing else to be discovered, they asked the landlady if she knew where the three of them may have gone. First, she was surprised to learn that they were gone. Then she was surprised to learn there were three of them. She said that they told her they were from Ransom, Kansas, when they moved in, so as far as she knew, they went home without telling her.

To clarify, Big Jim asked, "They didn't say Sedalia, Missouri? You're sure?"

She was certain, but checked her rent book and it confirmed Ransom, Kansas.

From there, Big Jim, Edith, and Annie, who could identify the girls, and two police officers went to the bus station to search for the threesome. They later reported that they didn't see them and that there wasn't a bus scheduled to leave that night after the bus at 7 p.m. That bus was headed to Des Moines, Iowa, but Big Jim doubted they took it.

Meanwhile, Austin, Deloris, Gracie, and two more police officers went to Union Station. Deloris checked the train schedule and found that there was a train leaving for St. Louis at midnight. Austin directed the officers to check downstairs while he and Deloris walked around the main hall. Gracie headed for the ladies' room and searched, but didn't find anyone. Deloris headed for an obscure corner in the back of the massive hall and found one of the girls sitting there on a bench. Next to her was a large trunk that could hold a human being.

"Hello," Deloris began. The young woman looked up and

didn't seem to recognize her, so Deloris assumed this was Milly. "I don't believe we've met. You must be Milly."

At that, the young woman started to jump up, but Deloris blocked her. Deloris saw one officer coming up the stairs from the tracks and yelled for him to join her. He ran over and put handcuffs on Milly and guided her to the front of the hall. Deloris noticed that Austin and Gracie were closing in on another young woman sitting at a table in the empty Harvey lunch counter. She had her back to the door, oblivious to what was happening in the main hall. Deloris moved closer, but stood back while Austin approached her. He asked Gracie to hold back, too.

"Lilly," Austin said softly as he walked up to her.

"Austin! You found me." She looked up at him with a pleading in her eyes, before she saw Deloris over Austin's shoulder.

Austin said, "Yes, Lilly. I found you. We need for you and your sisters to come down to police headquarters and answer some questions. Do you know where we will find your sister Tilly or your other sister Milly?"

"Sisters?"

"Yes, we know now that there are three of you," Austin replied.

Deloris came closer and interrupted, "We found Milly over there." She pointed to Milly, who was standing with the police officer by her side. Gracie walked up too.

"Hello, Lilly," she greeted.

"Gracie? Oh." Lilly groaned as she realized Gracie was how they knew she was a triplet.

"Correction, then. Do you know where Tilly is?" Austin

persisted.

"I–I don't."

"I'm sorry, but you need to come with me," and he gently took her arm and helped her up. Then put the handcuffs on her.

"Do you really need to handcuff me?" Lilly asked.

"I'm afraid that I do." Austin replied.

"Are you with the police, Deloris?" Lilly asked.

"Oh, Lilly. No." Deloris shook her head, then remembered that there was a women's restroom on the bottom floor of the station. "I need to go. I thought of something."

She left Austin, Gracie, and Lilly standing there and rushed downstairs. Austin motioned for another officer to go with her.

Before she opened the door, Deloris heard water running inside and put her finger to her lips. "Shhh."

When she opened the door, there was a shuffling, as if someone ran to an empty stall and closed the door. "Tilly! We know you are in here. We already have Milly and Lilly in custody. You might as well give yourself up."

"Who are you? I don't know what you are talking about," came a voice from behind the door. "My name is Patricia."

"Tilly, we know it is you. Please come out. Otherwise, this police officer who is with me will need to break the door down and he really doesn't want to do that."

After a few minutes had passed, the lock on the door clicked and Tilly came walking out. She fought the officer putting handcuffs on her at first and then finally relented.

"It's you? Who *are* you?" Tilly asked Deloris incredulously.

"Just a concerned citizen who happened to like Sam Sloan."

"Figures."

Final Chapter

Wrap up

Lilly, Milly, and Tilly were all booked on suspicion of murder. Apparently, Tilly was the mastermind who cooked up the scheme to kill Sam and steal the coin. The coin was found in the package mailed to Sedalia, along with the bloody dress that Tilly wore when she killed Sam.

The coin was the main purpose for the entire scheme. It belonged to the Rossi family and had been in the family for centuries, brought to the United States when the Rossi girls' grandfather immigrated from Italy. It was worth millions of dollars and was to be their inheritance before their father foolishly gambled it away. Growing up, the girls' father showed them the coin many times and told them it was worth a fortune. He had been so proud of their family's legacy and the one thing he could give them. Ashamed that he lost the family fortune all in one night, their father committed suicide. The girls vowed revenge for their father's death and to retrieve the coin.

Tilly convinced her sisters to come to Kansas City, but that one of them needed to stay out of sight. They agreed Milly would do that. Tilly was the dominant triplet and historically bullied the other two girls since childhood. She had a beautiful face, but an ugly soul. According to those that knew her, she was vindictive and conniving.

Tilly picked the town of Ransom, Kansas, ahead of time because it was in the opposite direction from Sedalia and deep in the state of Kansas. She knew that the chances of the police traveling there to search for them would be slim in the beginning if they figured everything out and asked the landlady. Tilly tried to steal the coin from Sam several times when they were out on a date, but never succeeded. That's when she put Plan B into action: murder. Her sisters thought they were just going to steal the coin back and didn't know she planned to murder Sam until they found out that she killed him that night. They thought she was just going to knock him out and steal the coin.

Working at the dress shop, Tilly deliberately arranged for several women to be wearing the same dress in dark colors to the charity ball. Some wore lace capes, and some wore silk capes with the dress to give the appearance of unique looks. While the dress that Milly wore had sequins, that obviously didn't match the others or what anyone would see if Tilly was spotted leaving. She talked Connie Binaggio into changing her hairstyle and color to look like her own hair and left tips where Sam's ex-wives could find him at different places. She helped them both with their dresses and appearances, too. The stage was set for several people to attend the ball, looking very similar.

The night at the charity ball, Milly was actually the one singing on the stage and Tilly was the one downstairs stabbing Sam. Milly's scream was genuine because she didn't know her sister was planning to kill Sam.

The girls' mother convinced the authorities that Sam had stolen the coin from her husband, and she received the coin back. She sold it and used the money to hire the best defense lawyers that money could buy for her daughters. Consequently, Milly and Lilly convinced the jury that they didn't know their sister planned to murder Sam, and as a result, they each received a lighter sentence.

Alice Sloan retrieved her mother's brooch and put it in a safe deposit box. At Sam's funeral, she was the loudest mourner and garnered the most attention from attendees who gave her their condolences. She was still in love with Sam and only threatened to kill him with no intention of going through with it, when detectives asked her about it.

Austin took Lilly's betrayal a little hard, but was glad their relationship wasn't a long one. He remained a little guarded from that day forward in his love life. However, one good thing came out of this case; he made amends with Carolyn Bechtel, and they started dating. Austin and Big Jim received a bonus and accolades for cracking the murder case, but they knew it wouldn't have happened that early without Deloris, Annie, and Gracie. With their bonuses, they took everyone at the boarding house, even Thelma's daughters and Leota, out to eat at the Savoy Grill.

Annie received an award for her reporting of the Christopher Columbus Charity Ball and the murder investigation. She started dating one of the officers who was with her at the bus station.

Gracie finished her semester in chemistry and everything became easier for her and Edith, living in the same house.

Deloris still worked at the switchboard and Indiana Gardens through the winter of 1931-1932 and when Poppy's opened back up, she went back there for the summer season working weekends and worked at Indiana Gardens off and on through the week. She also continued dating two fellows, Leon and Les.

One last thing. Tilly had tracked down Sam with the help

of Julius T. Stanford III, who pretended to be jealous of Sam taking Tilly from him. Jules heard that the server at the Riverside Club was friends with Sam and was involved in fleecing some of the patrons, so he set him up to tell Sam his whereabouts that first night. It was a reverse Kansas City Shuffle.

Jules was arrested for accessory to murder, but was found not guilty and released. His daddy hired an expensive lawyer who proved that Jules had no idea why Tilly wanted Sam or that she planned to kill him. He didn't even know there were three girls. It was a reverse, reverse Kansas City Shuffle on both Sam Sloan and Jules Stanford.

Food Terms Used

almond praline semifreddo with grappa and poached apricots: a half-frozen dessert that is a cross between ice cream and mousse.

broccolini: a sweet and mild cross between broccoli and Chinese broccoli that belongs to the cabbage family.

broccoli rabe: bold and bitter vegetable that is leafier, thinner, and less floral than broccoli.

cannoncini: Italian cream horns pastry filled with Chantilly cream.

cannoli: a tube-shaped pastry filled with sweet ricotta cheese, whipping cream, and powdered sugar.

chocolate budino: similar to pudding, but thicker.

ciambella: a ring-shaped cake.

gagootz: a type of squash commonly called zucchini or courgetti, also known as cucuzza, an Italian summer squash, that is slightly sweet with a firm texture and is long and green.

radicchio: a red type of leafy chicory.

sfogliatelle ricce: a type of pastry that is sometimes called "lobster tail pastry" from its shape.

soffritto: known as the holy trinity of Italian cooking; the base for many Italian dishes and is made with celery, onions and carrots.

struffolis: deep fried dough balls coated with honey also known as honey balls, stacked one upon another in a circle.

sugo: basic tomato sauce used on spaghetti or pasta.

Italian words and slang

Che peccato: Too bad

Ciao: Hello and Goodbye

Chiudere il becco: Shut up. Literally close the beak.

Delizioso: Delicious

Famiglia: Family

Gagootz: Also known as cucuzza it also describes a person who is crazy in the head.

G-men: Slang for Government men, Federal Prohibition Agents. Eliot Ness and his untouchables were G-men.

Goombah: Male friends, buddies

Lug Tax: Money paid by honest Italian business owners to have a promise from the mafia that they will not be harmed or their business will not be torched.

Malfattore: Criminal, delinquent, malevolent
Non capisco: Don't understand

Omerta: Death. In the mafia it is the code or vow of silence or else death.

Pacca sul sedere: A term used when Italian men pinch a beautiful woman on her backside.

Rallentare: Slowdown
Rischiosa: Risky

Squisito: Exquisite

Gambling Term

Twenty-six: dice game popular in the Midwestern United States from the 1920s through the 1950s, in which a player selects a number from 1 to 6 and then casts 10 dice 13 times, attempting to throw the chosen number 26 times or more, or exactly 13 times, or fewer than 10 times. The house edge (advantage) in this game is approximately 18 percent. https://www.britannica.com/topic/twenty-six

Additional Information

¹Eids of March coin description came from Wikipedia

Deloris Markham aka Doris O'Meara: My mother, Doris Markham, really did change her name to Doris O'Meara when she was arrested in a raid by G-men at her work. She also worked at the Indiana Gardens Restaurant.

Indiana Gardens versus Italian Gardens: There really was a restaurant named Indiana Gardens. It only lasted a few years and has been lost to history. It should not be confused with the Italian Gardens Restaurant that was open for several decades.

Angelo & Sicilia Martinelli: Are false names but represent real people. Yes, Angelo really did hide liquor in a safe and yes, the feds really did put water in a glass that held alcohol to get enough liquid to arrest him during Prohibition.

Columbus Day, October 11, 1931: Kansas City's Italian community really did celebrate Columbus Day on October 11th and had all of the events I listed, including the ball at Vacarro Hall. There was no murder there, however.

Miss Markham Mysteries
BOOK FOUR

Wheels Up Aviator Down

Prologue: September 11, 1932

Friday nights at the Indiana Gardens Italian Restaurant in Kansas City were usually busy for the waitresses, and Deloris was just taking a customer's order when four women walked in. One of them Deloris recognized right away from her short hair, easygoing smile and the slacks she was wearing. Very few women wore trousers, which this woman was famous for wearing. Deloris had seen her picture in the newspaper just the other day. She was planning to fly solo across the Atlantic Ocean from Newfoundland to Ireland in a few weeks.

Here was one of the most famous people, a woman—Amelia Earhart, and she was seated in Deloris's station. Besides Amelia, the second woman had an air of authority about her and was dressed in a business type suit. She was obviously in charge. The third woman wore loose trousers and had her medium brown hair cut short and straight like Amelia. The fourth woman was very stylish, dressed to the nines in a frilly dress, high heels, heavy on the makeup and her blonde hair was in short curls.

As Deloris brought them each a glass of water, she overheard a part of their conversation.

"You found what?" the second woman asked.

"My great, great grandmother's diary from when my family traveled west in a covered wagon," the third woman replied.

"How exciting," the fourth woman spoke up. "Where did you find it?"

"I found it behind a brick in the basement of my grandmother's home. She told me about it right before she died, but don't tell anyone else. I need you to keep my secret until I can read it," the third one implored. "I just found it last night and none of my family knows about it yet."

Deloris interrupted before anyone could answer. "Hello. Welcome to Indiana Gardens. What would you like to drink?"

"I'll have a Coke," Amelia said.

The second woman responded, "I'll have a 7up."

"Me too," the fourth woman answered, smiling at Jackie.

The last one ordered water. Deloris left to get their drinks. When she returned, she placed the drinks in front of them. She took their food order. After they finished eating, Deloris went back to the table. "Excuse me, but aren't you, Amelia Earhart?"

"Yes, I am," Amelia said proudly.

"I read about you in the paper. You flew solo across the Atlantic?"

"Yes, I did," Amelia replied.

"How exciting," Deloris gushed.

The second woman then spoke up. "Well, you obviously recognize Amelia, and my name is Jackie Cochran. This is

Harriett Davidson," she pointed to the third woman. "But she goes by Harry and that one over there admiring herself in her mirror," indicating the fourth woman, "Is Betsy McGuire. We are all fly girls now."

"Really? That is amazing," Deloris said with obvious admiration. Deloris started to say something else, but saw Stella motion to her that more customers just walked in and it was Deloris's turn to serve them. "Oh, I guess I need to take care of those customers." She left to serve them and then came back to Amelia, Jackie, Harry and Betsy and asked. "Can I get you a dessert or anything else?"

"We are celebrating. How about we have some dessert?" Amelia asked the group, and they all agreed except Betsy, who was distractedly checking her makeup in her mirror.

"What are you celebrating?" Deloris questioned.

Amelia answered, "Well, Harry and Betsy there, just passed their pilot licenses and Jackie over there passed her pilot's license last month, doing it in a record time of only three weeks. She then proceeded to fly 350 miles into Canada, setting a record for distance and crossing international lines."

"And Amelia flew across the Atlantic!" Jackie quickly spoke up. "This is the first chance we've all had to gather and celebrate."

"So, I want something special. What do you recommend?" Amelia asked, not acknowledging Jackie's accolades.

"Almond Praline Semifreddo with Grappa is our specialty," Deloris answered.

The three nodded, then looked at Betsy for her reply. "What?" she responded, looking up at everyone staring at her.

"Do you want dessert?" Harry questioned.

"Oh dessert, yes please," Betsy replied.

Laughing, Amelia spoke up, "How about an order of that then for each of us and the bill is on me?"

As Deloris returned with the dessert, she eagerly stated, "I think flying a plane must be very exciting."

"We all agree with you," Amelia nodded her head in approval.

"Jackie got her wings in only three weeks," Betsy spoke up, looking at Jackie with pride.

"Amelia already told her that," Harry spoke up, shaking her head in amusement.

"Oh," Betsy said as she put her mirror back in her purse, looking embarrassed.

"Well, I was determined to get my pilot's license quickly," Jackie added. "So, I could start selling my own makeup brand all over the United States." She then turned to Amelia and said, "I think I will go ahead and quit at Antoine's Hair Salon. I took a six-week vacation to learn to fly."

"You sell makeup?" Deloris asked, a little confused.

"Oh, you ought to try it," Betsy interrupted. "It is the best. And now that I have my wings, I'm going to help her sell it."

When Amelia handed Deloris the money for the bill, she said, "Well, I'd better get going. I've got a plane to catch." Everyone laughed at her comment and the group stood up to leave, lingering to hug and say goodbye to each other.

Deloris returned to the kitchen and told Nina and Stella

about the four women. When Deloris returned to the dining hall, Harry and Betsy were still standing at the table talking.

Deloris walked up to the table to clear it off, when Harry asked, "Would you like to go up in a plane sometime?"

"Would I? Yes!" Deloris almost screamed.

"I can take you, too, now that I have my wings," Betsy offered.

"That sounds amazing. Here is my telephone number and address. I work mornings at a switchboard and weekend nights here, but I am free all other times," Deloris said.

"Okay toots, you're on. Meet me at the Fairfax Airport Sunday at 12 noon," Harry offered.

"I'll be there," Deloris replied excitedly.

As they exited the building, Deloris could hear Betsy say, "What are you going to do about you know who?" She said the last part in almost a whisper.

"I don't know," Harriet replied. "But I'll figure something out."

About the Author

My name is Debby Dilks, although I am trying to become accustomed to using my given name Deborah Dilks again. I was born and raised in Northwest Missouri, moving to the Greater Kansas City area when I graduated from high school and staying after I married. My husband and I have been married for over 50 years. We have two children, five grandchildren and a host of other people whom we consider a part of our family, from past foreign exchange students and their families to my former college students and their families.

When I retired from working at the University of Missouri-Kansas City, I focused upon completing a book about my mother that I started in 2011 while working full time. My mother believed in me and my writing. She inspired me to write a book about her life while she was alive, but I just wasn't able to do that. Now I have accomplished that goal with two biographies of her life: *Miss Kansas City Kitty: Doris Markham's Story* and *Mrs. Kansas City Kitty: Doris Swinney and Family*. A friend suggested we write cozy mysteries loosely based upon my mother's life, and that is when the Miss Markham Mysteries series started, with Deloris Markham, an amateur sleuth, solving one crime after another. My mother didn't solve murder mysteries, but I am confident she would totally embrace this series because she was spunky like Deloris.

To date, in early 2025, I have written three historical biographies, one cozy mystery, and one short story under my name. I co-wrote under the pseudonym Juliet E. Sidonie with my friend two cozy mysteries and one short story. There are at least ten more books planned to be written in the Miss Markham Mystery series, and two books about UMKC.

Sadly, because of circumstances beyond her control, my friend will not be continuing to co-write with me in the Miss Markham Mystery series, but I will continue under my own name. I hope I can provide you with the same enjoyment in the future books that you have experienced with the first two.

DeborahDilks.com and MissMarkhamMysteries.com
Click on QR code for future events or to order books:

Please rate my books on both Amazon and Goodreads - Deborah Dilks or Juliet E. Sidonie.

If you and your group or book club would like me to come and speak to you about the books, please send me a message on Messenger through Deborah E. Dilks, Writer on Facebook or email: delorismarkham09@gmail.com

Facebook: Deborah E. Dilks, Writer

Instagram: debby_dilks

X: @DDilks3

Or

Facebook: Juliet Sidonie or Juliet Sidonie, Author

Instagram: julietsidonie

X: @JulietSidonie

Other Miss Markham Mysteries Books by Juliet E. Sidonie

Two cozy mystery books in the *Miss Markham Mystery* series

Murder Among Friends

Peculiarities at the Picnic

"Mystery of the Missing Heirloom" in *Six Spooky Stories, A Halloween Cozy Collection*

Other Books by Deborah Dilks

Miss Kansas City Kitty Doris Markham's Story

Mrs. Kansas City Kitty Doris Swinney and Family

From World War II to the Run of the Year

The Kansas City Shuffle, A Miss Markham Mystery Book Three

"Jameson and Pattonsburg" in the collection *Lye Soap and Sad Irons: A Living History of Northwest Missouri*